MILK OF HUMAN KINDNESS

MILK OF HUMAN KINDNESS

Elizabeth Ferrars

Chivers Press • G.K. Hall & Co.
Bath, England   Thorndike, Maine USA

This Large Print edition is published by Chivers Press, England, and by G.K. Hall & Co., USA.

Published in 1997 in the U.K. by arrangement with Constable & Company Limited.

Published in 1997 in the U.S. by arrangement with Harold Ober Associates, Inc.

U.K. Hardcover ISBN 0–7451–6950–3 (Chivers Large Print)
U.K. Softcover   ISBN 0–7451–6962–7 (Camden Large Print)
U.S. Softcover   ISBN 0–7838–1968–4 (Nightingale Collection Edition)

The text of this Large Print edition is unabridged.
Other aspects of the book may vary from the original edition.

Set in 16 pt. New Times Roman.

Printed in Great Britain on acid-free paper.

British Library Cataloguing in Publication Data available

Library of Congress Cataloging-in-Publication Data

Ferrars, Elizabeth, 1907–
    Milk of human kindness / Elizabeth Ferrars.
        p.   cm.
    ISBN 0–7838–1968–4 (lg. print : sc)
    1. Large type books.   I. Title.
    [PR6003.R458M55   1997]
    823'.912—dc20   96–30931
                                                                              CIP

It is too full of the milk of human
kindness...

MACBETH

CHAPTER ONE

I always have mixed feelings about an unexpected ring at the doorbell, and this is particularly so on a Sunday morning, when the ring is unlikely to mean a tradesman who can be dealt with in a minute or two.

The trouble is that just occasionally, when one warily opens the door, one finds the one person in the whole world whom one really wants to see at that moment, and so it is difficult to stick to good resolutions about not opening doors, even if one happens to be occupied with serious matters.

Really, I think all front-doors should be fitted with periscopes attached to the fanlights, so that one can see who is waiting outside. I am sure that if I had been able to see who was outside, ringing my bell again and again with a rather offensive impatience on a certain Sunday morning last September, I should never have gone to the door. By this I should have been saved a great deal of trouble and disturbance and perhaps should have saved a life. I am not absolutely certain about that last point, but still I think that I should like a periscope.

John was away on that Sunday. He had gone to Holland for a fortnight to a conference of some sort, and I had decided, while he was

1

gone, to do something about the flat. So I had got in tins of distemper and paint and some brushes and turpentine, and had spent Saturday evening mixing colours, meaning to get off to a good start in the morning. The good start had not actually been made, because having no one else for whom to cook breakfast, I had stayed in bed a good deal longer than I had intended, and then had sat over my coffee, reading the film-reviews and the fashion bits and the advertisements in the Sunday paper, until it almost looked as if it might not be worth while beginning work till after lunch. That meant that I should have to get dressed and go out before I could start, because I consider that it is completely impossible to cook only for oneself, and so had not bothered to buy anything the day before but some bread and some coffee. All my meals except breakfast I was going to have at the Greek place down the street. It was while I was at the stage of wondering if I could bear to leave the gas-fire to go to the bathroom and get washed, that the door-bell rang.

I had not the faintest idea who it could be, and my first instinct was to freeze until the caller went away. But then, for no particular reason, I became convinced that it was Peter Frere. He knew that I was alone and he had said something about picking me up for a drink some time. Peter is tall, admirably muscular and a notable handyman. In a flash I saw him

2

climbing competently on chairs, taking down curtains and pictures, moving heavy bookcases and rolling up carpets. I went to the door.

It served me right. It was Susan, my sister.

She looked at me with a contemptuous wrinkling of her handsome nose and said, 'Not dressed yet?'

I said, 'It's Sunday.'

'I got up at half past seven.'

'I hope you enjoyed it,' I said.

'Aren't you going to ask me to come in?'

I suppose I had been standing there looking as if I were deliberately barring her way in. One's attitudes so often give away more of what one is feeling than one intends that they should.

As I got out of the way, Susan walked in, went straight into the sitting-room and said, 'What a filthy mess.'

'John's away,' I explained.

'You mean it's John who cleans up?'

'Well, he helps, of course,' I said. 'But I meant that it doesn't seem worth while cleaning up just for myself.'

'I don't know how you can stand it.'

To me it had not seemed as bad as all that. The cushions had not been shaken up, the ash-trays had not been emptied and there were probably a few crumbs on the carpet. Apart from that, there was only a newspaper spread out on the floor in the middle of the room with some tins of paint on it, some brushes soaking

3

in a jam-jar of turpentine, and a big tin of distemper which I had begun to stir with an old wooden spoon that I had decided to sacrifice for the purpose. But those things were work, not mess.

Yet when Susan walked into the room, it did in some way begin to seem more unkempt than I had realised. She was able to make almost any room seem frayed and shabby and unworthy of her, for she always carried a natural splendour about with her. If rich carpets had spread themselves wherever she set her feet, if thrones had supplied themselves when she wanted to sit down, it would only have seemed proper. She always made me think of sumptuous furnishing. For one thing, she always looked as if she herself had been newly upholstered that day in some fresh creamy, velvety skin and some brand-new golden hair. In fact, she is a beauty. She was even more of a beauty at forty than she had been at thirty or twenty.

That morning she was wearing a casual tweed suit and a small felt hat to match, some stitched leather gloves and low-heeled tan shoes. If I had worn these things, she would have asked me why on earth I was going horsey, but I could not ask her that because on her there was nothing horsey about them. Not that they would have looked horsey on me either, but she would have said that they did, and I should have hated them from that

4

day on.

Sitting down on a small chair in a corner of the room, as if by doing that she ran least risk of being damaged by contact with the mess, she asked me, 'Where's John gone to?'

'Holland,' I said.

'What for?'

'Some conference or other.'

'How long will he be gone?'

'A fortnight. Was it John you came to see?'

She shook her head. 'As a matter of fact, it makes it easier if he's away. But aren't you going to give me something to eat? I'm ravenous.'

'You shouldn't have breakfast so early,' I said. 'It's not economic.'

'Well, for God's sake get me something.'

'I can get you some coffee, but there's nothing to eat in the place,' I said.

'Why, what are you going to have yourself?' she asked.

'I'm going out to eat.'

'You shouldn't, it's bad for you, you never know what you're getting.'

'I don't mind, so long as I really don't know.'

'Well, let's open a tin of something,' she said, getting up and going to the kitchen. 'I can't last much longer.'

'You'll get fat, eating between meals,' I said.

'Don't be silly, nothing makes me fat—' She stood still in the doorway of the kitchen. 'Good Lord, when did you wash up last?'

There were only the things from yesterday's supper and breakfast there, which I did not think was bad when one was alone, so I did not trouble to answer.

Susan went to the cupboard where she knew I kept my tins, and looked inside. 'Spaghetti,' she said. 'I don't like tinned spaghetti.'

'I didn't buy it for you,' I said.

'Haven't you any pork and beans? I like pork and beans.'

'No.'

'And I quite like pilchards.'

'I don't. I haven't any pilchards.'

She turned and looked at me with a puzzled expression in her big, brown eyes. 'Marabelle, what's wrong?'

'Nothing's wrong—so far.'

'But you don't seem glad to see me.' Reaching into the cupboard, she added absently, 'This'll have to do.' She began to open a tin of sardines. 'Something *is* wrong,' she went on. 'I can always tell. You're upset about something.'

I said nothing.

'You *are* upset,' she said. 'It isn't anything I've done, is it? I hope not, because I came here to ask you to do something for me.'

'That's what I thought,' I said.

She found the loaf of bread, cut a couple of slices and put them under the grill. 'Want some too?' she asked hospitably.

'No thanks.'

6

'You see,' she said, giving me a quick look, then looking back at the toast browning, 'a rather horrible thing has happened to me.'

As she said it her forehead wrinkled and her voice became uncertain. She turned the two pieces of bread with a jerky movement that did not seem characteristic of her.

'Well,' I said, 'tell me.'

'Sure you won't have something to eat?'

'All right then—one piece.'

She cut another slice of bread. The loaf was only a small one, and I began to wonder if it would last out till my breakfast next day. We put the sardines on the toast and took them to the sitting-room, where Susan sat down close to the fire and ate with close attention. All of a sudden she seemed not to want to say any more.

As she chased a few remaining crumbs of oily toast round her plate with a rosily manicured fingernail, I asked, 'Feeling better now?'

She nodded, licked the finger, and avoiding my eyes, said, 'I don't know where to begin. You're sure to tell me it serves me right.'

'Let's assume that said.'

'Well, it's Norman ... He's gone quite queer, and without any explanation.'

That was not what I had expected. She had married Norman Rice, had two children by him, been divorced by him and had two husbands since, all without a cross word

7

spoken. It had seemed a triumph in human relationships.

'What's he done?' I asked. 'He isn't getting married again, is he?'

'I wish he were,' she said, 'provided it was the right sort of person—and probably it wouldn't be. Poor Norman, he does need such a lot of looking after. I've tried for years and years to get him to marry again. But I don't think that's what it is. I mean, I don't see why that should make any difference between him and me.'

Nor did I, as a matter of fact, except that wives are sometimes unreasonable people. The new one, for instance, might have an inclination to cut Susan's throat.

'But what's he actually done?' I asked again.

'He won't let me see the children.'

'Oh ....'

She looked at me and nodded intensely.

I thought about it for a moment, then asked, 'I suppose you haven't misinterpreted something he's said?'

'Not a chance.'

'But you had Beryl staying with you only last month.'

'I know, and she did so enjoy it.' Beryl is Susan's eighteen-year-old daughter. 'I got her some lovely clothes and cut her hair off. I think she's going to be as good-looking as I am.'

'Did that have something to do with it—the new clothes, I mean?'

'I don't see why. When she got home again

Norman wrote to say how lovely she was looking. He wrote in quite his usual sort of way. And then last Wednesday he came to see me. That's when the queerness started. He sent a telegram to say he was coming, but it only came about an hour before he was due, and unluckily I was out. But Piers was in and saw him.' Piers Beltane was Number Three, Susan's Jane Seymour, very dearly beloved for the present, at least as far as I could tell. 'Poor Piers simply couldn't cope at all. Of course, you know what he's like—I'm sure he didn't really trouble to try and understand what Norman was saying. All Piers told me when I got home was that Norman had been up and didn't seem to want me to see him or the children any more. Piers seemed to think it quite natural and simply wouldn't bother his head about it.'

'Perhaps he was even a little glad.'

'Oh no.' She rushed to his defence. 'Piers isn't mean. He wouldn't be glad about anything that made me unhappy.'

The odd thing is that none of Susan's husbands are ever mean or ever want anything that would make her unhappy. I have no idea whether she achieves this by education or by picking the right material in the first place.

'Why don't you go down to see Norman yourself, and find out what it's all about?' I asked.

'I've been,' she said.

9

'When?'

'Yesterday.' Her fingers closed tightly round her handkerchief and tore at it. It was the first sign she had given of anger rather than mere bewilderment. 'He wouldn't see me.'

'That doesn't sound like Norman.'

'That's what I thought. I thought it didn't sound one little bit like Norman. And that's why I began to wonder ....'

'Did you see Beryl or Maurice?'

She shook her head.

'Whom did you see?'

She did not answer directly, but prodding with one of her pointed finger-nails at a small tear in the loose cover of the chair she was sitting in, she asked in a soft, smooth voice, 'Marabelle, tell me your candid opinion of Mrs Fawcett.'

Before I had had time to think, I laughed.

Susan, not quite so smoothly, went on rapidly, 'There's nothing funny about it. That kind of quiet, sly, meek, little woman can be extraordinarily dangerous. I know when I engaged her I thought she seemed a very nice sort of person, but I admit one can easily make mistakes about that sort of thing. Look at Mrs Grange, who seemed so very respectable and then stole all that linen. And Miss Pinker, of all people, having an illegitimate baby at the age of forty-five. Oh, one can make mistakes.'

I nodded. Recapitulated like that, it seemed that Susan's insistence on engaging housekeepers for Norman during the past ten years had not been without its disadvantages for him. But for the last two months she had been insisting that Mrs Fawcett was the perfect answer to his needs. I had seen her only once, and had formed no opinion about her except that she cooked abominably.

'Was it Mrs Fawcett who told you that Norman wouldn't see you?' I asked.

'Yes, and she said it on the doorstep, of all intolerable insults. She pretended to be very apologetic, and to blame it all on Norman, saying it was his orders that I was not to be received in the house. But I could see the satisfaction it gave her to say it. I saw all of a sudden how intensely she resented me and what real pleasure it gave her to be able to keep me out of the house. My own house! It did make me wonder if—well, if she wasn't getting Norman into her clutches somehow.'

I suppose I am so used to Susan and her point of view that it did not occur to me to point out that that house was not exactly her own. 'And where do I come in?' I asked.

But I knew already, and sure enough, in a moment Susan was reaching out a hand, laying it on my knee, pressing it affectionately and looking appealingly into my eyes.

'All I want is to understand what the trouble is,' she said. 'What I can't bear is this feeling of a bolt from the blue that's knocked me dizzy without my being able to make out what it's all

11

about. I must see the children, Marabelle, I must, I love them. Or at any rate—that's what I really meant to say—I must understand why Norman's done this. It's so unfair, and as you said, it isn't like him. I'm terribly worried, and even a bit frightened. Norman's always liked you, Marabelle...'

I looked at my paint-pots, my brushes, my turpentine, I looked at the walls of the room. They were of a grimy off-white of which I was dreadfully tired. Thinking about the peculiar and interesting shade of pink that I had mixed so carefully the evening before, I said, 'I don't see why Norman should let me in any more than you.'

'But of course he would,' said Susan. 'He's got a tremendously high opinion of you—and of John. He'd never insult you as he did me. After all, I'm only his divorced wife, he can do what he likes to me and I've no right to complain. But you're a person of some importance, a successful dramatist. He's proud of his connection with you. I've heard him say so. Of course he'd let you in.'

Whenever Susan remembered that I had once written a play which had been performed at no profit to me by a Sunday Society, I knew that she must really be in a very bad way indeed. But I did think there was something curious in Norman's behaviour, and even, considering the situation that he had allowed to persist for so long, rather unfair to Susan.

12

But before I could say so, she went on, 'As a matter of fact, I'm wondering if Norman's quite well. Mrs Fawcett said something about his stomach and his having to have priority milk ... I've been worrying over that as well.'

I was not sure if she threw that in as a make-weight to move my sympathies or whether her worry was genuine. It might have been, for illness always moved Susan deeply. She was at the service of any one who was ill, as Piers Beltane had rapidly discovered. He had made his marriage very comfortable for himself with a slight touch of asthma.

'Well, all right, I'll go,' I said, 'and see what I can find out. But I don't promise to get him to change his decision. I never was much good at exerting influence.'

'You'll go to-day?' she asked eagerly.

I looked round at the walls. There was time to put on one coat of paint that afternoon. 'To-morrow,' I said.

'To-day. Please, Marabelle.'

'The Sunday trains are awful.'

'There's quite a good one at four-ten.'

'To-morrow,' I said.

She stood up. She seemed satisfied. Putting a hand on my shoulder she said, 'I knew I could count on you.'

'And now,' I said, 'I think I'd better start getting dressed.'

'Yes—yes, of course, I'll go.' But her manner, now that she had achieved what she

13

wanted, had immediately become strangely absent. For a moment I had an uncomfortable suspicion that there was something more behind all this than she had said. Perhaps she saw the look. She explained, 'I was just wondering if it would be a good idea to have some more sardines on toast. But I suppose I'd better be getting home to tell Piers it's all right. He said he knew you'd go if I put it to you the right way.' She leant towards me, kissed me, and hurried out before there was any risk of my changing my mind.

CHAPTER TWO

And after all, I went by the four-ten. By the time that I had had lunch I had begun to feel that since I was committed to the business, it was best to get it over, and by going at once, I thought, I might even be able to catch a late train home that evening and make a good start on my decorating next day. All the same, having no trust in Sunday trains and recognising that Norman might take a little handling, I packed a small bag.

I had just remembered to turn off the Ascot, and was feeling proud of myself for that, when Susan rang up to ask me when I was going. I told her that I was leaving immediately. She said an odd thing. 'Bless you, my dear—I'll write you a letter to-night.' It worried me. Susan never writes letters.

Norman lived at Leckham, about two hours journey from Victoria. It was nearly dark when I got there. Before leaving the station, I studied the time-table and found that the last train back to London left Leckham at eight-seven. That meant that I should almost certainly have to stay there the night, so in case Norman received me as he had received Susan, not letting me get further than his doorstep, I decided to take certain precautions. Instead of telling the taxi-driver to take me straight to the Rices' house, I told him to stop at the bungalow next door to it, which belonged to Ernst and Millie Weinkraut.

Millie opened the door to me. She was a slim, grey-haired, untidy woman of about forty-five, with a sallow skin, absent-minded grey eyes, a passionate but indiscriminating interest in old furniture, and a high, faintly cockney voice.

'Why, look who's here,' she said. 'Ernie, Ernie—look who's here.' The grey eyes smiled at me kindly without quite bringing their attention to bear upon me. 'We've been talking about you,' she said. 'We were saying—what were we saying? I don't quite remember. It was some time ago. Quite a while ago really, I suppose. Ernie'—she called back over her shoulder—'what was it we were saying about Marabelle?'

'That it was time she and John should come

15

and see us, of course,' said Ernst, coming trotting out of the sitting-room. He was a short man, round-faced, bald and plump. He worked at Leckham Observatory, adored gardening and almost completely filled his acre of ground with roses, and in what time he had over, was writing a book on St Ambrose. He had been writing it for about fifteen years. His short, broad hand took hold of mine and broke it in two. 'Where's John?' he asked, peering past me into the darkness. 'No John?'

'He's in Holland,' I said.

Millie leant against the banisters and looked dreamily at an old carved chest that blocked up most of the little hall. Millie never stood up straight if she could lean against something. 'I knew we were talking about her,' she said. 'I was thinking about it only a little while ago. Funny the way one thinks of things and forgets them.'

'I've really come to see Norman,' I said, 'but I'd like to come in and talk to you first for a few minutes, if I may.'

'Ah, to see Norman—I think that is a goot idea,' Ernst's heavy guttural voice conveyed something that I did not understand, or so I thought. Really it might only have been that I had somehow slipped into a bad habit of mine, which is listening for overtones. 'Norman will be glad to see you, very glad.'

'That's the point,' I said, as they took me into their sitting-room. 'Will he?'

16

'But vy not?' said Ernst. 'Vy should he not be?'

'That's what I've come to talk about,' I said.

Their sitting-room was a square room with a low ceiling and a huge brick fireplace. Linoleum imitating red tiles covered the floor, while a collection of oak chests, mahogany bureaus and gate-legged tables blocked up almost every square inch of space. There were some comfortable chairs and there were several glass bowls on shelves and tables, which even at that time of year were full of roses. Ernst thought happily that the room looked supremely English, and Millie just loved it for itself.

I took a chair and was given a cigarette and a glass of sherry.

'And now vot is it viz Norman?' Ernst asked, propping the small of his back against the brick mantelpiece.

I had not thought out what to say. I had an idea that Susan might not like having her affairs unnecessarily discussed with the Weinkrauts, yet it was possible that they could be helpful.

'Is anything the matter with Norman, that you know of?' I asked cautiously.

'Well, it's funny that you should ask that,' said Millie, 'because Ernie and I were saying only the other day—what was it? Oh, I know. We were saying, something must be wrong with someone in the house, though nothing's

17

been said about it to us, because they're having priority milk. Ernie sees the bottles on the doorstep when he goes off to work in the mornings.'

'I wasn't meaning that exactly,' I said. 'I was meaning, is there anything queer that you've noticed about—well, Norman's behaviour, his temper and so on.'

Ernst looked thoughtful and did not answer. Millie thrust her fingers through her short, grey hair and gave her head a good scratch. Then she shook it.

'I haven't noticed anything,' she said.

Since I knew that Millie never noticed anything except advertisements for sales for furniture, I waited for what Ernst would say.

'Well,' he said at last, 'I am not sure.'

'That means there *is* something.'

'No, I have not noticed anyzing viz Norman. But viz the two young vuns, perhaps somezing.'

I waited again.

'But you are not interested in that,' he said, 'you vant to know about Norman.' This seemed to depress him.

'I'd like to know about anything queer that seems to be happening in the house,' I said.

'Oh, nothing is *happening*,' he said. 'And perhaps it is just that the young vuns are growing up, but somehow things feel different. There is a tension. I cannot describe it, but I know it when it comes.'

18

Millie shook her head. 'I haven't noticed anything,' she repeated, 'except that Beryl's got a lot of new clothes. I can't think why, she doesn't need them here.'

'But you ask all this for a purpose,' said Ernst.

I could not help the feeling that whatever that purpose might be, he had decided to tell me as little as possible about Norman. That made me sure for the first time that there was something to tell.

'Well, if I go over there now,' I said, 'd'you think there's any risk that Norman will shut the door in my face?'

'Good heavens,' said Ernst, 'vy should he do that?' He sounded genuinely surprised at the question.

I went on, 'He hasn't said anything during the last few days to suggest that he might possibly do such a thing?'

Ernst shook his heavy head emphatically.

'If he does anything crazy like that,' Millie remarked, 'you can always come back here.'

'Thanks, I was rather hoping for that,' I said.

'But this is strange,' said Ernst, 'most strange. I cannot think vy you should ask this question.'

'Anyway, I'm glad you think it'll be all right,' I said.

'You have not done something to annoy him?' said Ernst. 'You have not, for instance, made him a character in a new play you

19

are writing?'

'I'm not writing any play,' I said.

'What do you do with yourself then?'

'At the moment I'm redecorating the flat.'

Millie looked interested. 'Really? D'you know, I've thought of trying my hand at that. I've never done any, but there's a lot of scope in it, isn't there? Perhaps we could have a talk about it. You could give me advice.'

Ernst quickly took me by the arm. 'Perhaps you go now and see what Norman has to say to you,' he said. 'Then if he vill not see you, which I cannot imagine, you come back here for supper and tell us all about the next play you vill write. It vill be very interesting to hear all about it—more than about house-painting.'

'I'm not going to write another,' I said.

'Nonsense,' he said, 'one always writes another. It is much better than house-painting. Now I take you through the garden.' Taking no notice of Millie's look of frustration, he drove me out of the room ahead of him. Outside now it was quite dark, a cool, cloudy night with a pleasant, damp, country smell in the air. Ernst took me across the lawn to the hedge between the two gardens. There was a noticeable gap in it, quite easy to pass through, with the twigs wrenching only one or two holes in one's stockings. He went with me as far as the path that circled the other house, then wished me good luck and turned back. I walked along to the porch and rang the

20

heavy doorbell.

Almost at once the hall inside sprang into light. Through the coloured panes of the stained glass panels of the door, I saw the small, dark figure of a woman coming towards me. Because I was looking at her through the petticoat of a shepherd-girl in the panel, most of her face appeared purple and her hair cerise, but I could still recognise her as Mrs Fawcett, the housekeeper.

Half-way across the hall she paused uncertainly. She seemed to be peering towards the door. Then she took a few steps in the direction of Norman's study, but changing her mind, she turned back towards the entrance and opened the door.

Actually I did not care very much whether or not she let me in. If she turned me away, I should have done all that I had undertaken, and I should have been able to spend a quiet evening with the Weinkrauts. In fact, when I realised that Mrs Fawcett was smiling at me warmly and holding the door further open, I believe I felt some disappointment. To have a door shut in one's face is not in itself pleasant, but can save a lot of trouble.

She did not look surprised to see me, though her first words were, 'Well, what a surprise! Quite a stranger, aren't you?' Probably she would have said that, whatever the state of her feelings. Mrs Fawcett's vocabulary carried all her thoughts along certain well-defined grooves. 'Come in, my dear. Mr Rice will be so glad to see you.'

She was a very short woman, not much over five feet, and her age was just under sixty, though the deep wrinkles on her pale, square face, the thinness of her smooth grey hair, that showed the pink scalp through the rather greasy strands, and the hesitating slowness of her movements made her look older. But in the only conversation that we had ever had, she had discussed with me the intrigues she meant to start operating when she became eligible in a few months time for her old-age pension, so that she could still go on earning her present very high wages. She always wore a long, black, bunchy dress and felt slippers and she pottered slowly and unobtrusively about her work, doing extraordinarily little, yet managing to have herself regarded as a treasure. This was a sheer triumph of personality, because she was one of the worst cooks I have ever known, besides having insisted, when Susan engaged her for Norman, on having a char to do the housework.

Even on that first evening, as Mrs Fawcett let me in, it struck me that the char of the moment must be uncommonly efficient, for I had never seen the hall shine, one might almost say sparkle, as it did then. It was a big, square hall with a wide, carved staircase and a curly lamp-standard flowering out of the newel-post. All the woodwork was painted chocolate-brown. There was a Turkey carpet on the floor and over the doors there were antlers from East African animals, or so I have always supposed them to be, for East Africa was where Norman had spent his working life, though for all I knew, they might have been bought from the Army and Navy catalogue.

The house had been built by Norman's parents. Beside being hideous, it was cold and inconvenient. Susan had always refused absolutely to live there, which had struck me as one of her more reasonable decisions, and Norman himself had never thought of returning to it until it had occurred to him that it would make a good home for the children during the bombing of London. By the time the war ended he had settled down comfortably and would not hear of moving again. Norman, I should mention, was much older than Susan, twenty years, in fact. Because Susan had refused to live in East Africa, he had retired earlier than he had intended, and had spent the years since then with hobbies and rather disorganised studies.

When I saw him that evening, coming suddenly out of his study, saying that he had heard my voice in the hall, I was struck with surprise by the thought that he and Mrs Fawcett were the same age. She was such a desiccated old bundle, he was so wiry and alive. He was of medium height, thin and quick-moving, with a skin ruddy from long walks,

23

thick, white hair, blue, friendly eyes and a kind of whimsical distinction about him that attracted everybody. I suppose there are some serious disadvantages in being married to a man twenty years older than oneself; Norman himself, at any rate, had always assured me that there were; but I had always thought Susan mad to leave him.

He said to me, 'You'll be staying the night, of course. Mrs Fawcett, Mrs Baynes will be staying the night.'

'But she hasn't any luggage,' said Mrs Fawcett.

'I've a bag over at the Wienkrauts,' I said.

'We'll send Maurice over for it,' said Norman. 'Come along now and get warm and have some sherry. You can manage an extra person for dinner, Mrs Fawcett.'

'Oh yes, Mr Rice, I always manage,' said Mrs Fawcett with great self-satisfaction, and while my stomach shrank as I thought what that managing would probably mean, Norman beamed at her with astonishing pride of possession.

We went into the drawing-room and I had my second glass of sherry.

Norman drank with me, but I noticed that he only half-filled his glass and when he had taken a sip from it, put it down at some distance from him as if he intended to forget about it. That started me wondering about his health. He did not look ill. But his kind of dry, ruddy skin is unrevealing.

I did not know what to say, but sinking into a corner of the comfortable sofa, I smiled at him hopefully, thinking he must know why I had come, and that he had tact enough to handle the situation for me.

He smiled back.

'It's very nice to see you again,' he said. 'But tell me, where's John?'

I thought that before setting out I really ought to have written a card, saying, 'My husband is in Holland,' and pinned it to my lapel. It seemed that people were almost unable to believe in my existence apart from him. I told Norman where John was, adding, 'And you aren't surprised to see me, are you, Norman?'

'Since you've been left all alone at home? No, it was an excellent idea to come down here. I'm delighted you thought of it.'

'Only you know that had nothing to do with my coming.'

'No?'

'I don't think you'd ever be much good at looking deliberately stupid,' I said. 'You know why I've come.'

He looked as if he saw no reason to take this remark seriously. 'I'm delighted, whatever the reason may be,' he said, 'only I don't understand about the bag at the Weinkrauts. What made you leave it there?'

'Establishing a line of retreat in case I got

thrown out,' I said, 'as you had Susan thrown out yesterday.'

He gave me one of his quick, bright smiles.

'My dear, you are not Susan.'

CHAPTER THREE

He gave me a cigarette.

'I suppose,' he went on, making it sound casual, 'you've seen Susan?'

'This morning,' I said.

'I hope she wasn't much distressed.' The odd thing was that he seemed to mean it.

'She was very distressed,' I said.

He gave a slight, resigned shrug of his shoulders, as if to remind me that it is the human lot to suffer a certain amount of distress. 'A pity. I'm very sorry about it.'

'Then it's true,' I said, 'you did throw her out?'

His eyebrows went up. 'But I gathered she'd told you ....'

'Oh yes, she told me. But she has a way of dramatising things, hasn't she? I did think there might have been a certain amount of— well, exaggeration.'

'Not more than a little, anyway.'

'Well then, Norman, tell me what it's all about.'

He leant back, reached for his glass, and

looked as if he were thinking longingly of drinking what was left in it. Then he set it down again.

'We'll be having dinner in about ten minutes,' he said. 'Wouldn't you like to go up to your room and powder your nose, or whatever it is you do to yourself?'

'Yes, of course,' I said. 'But about Susan ....'

'Let's forget about Susan, shall we? You know, Marabelle, we've known each other since you were about fifteen years old, and we seem to have used our acquaintance for only one purpose, talking about Susan. Mightn't we find another subject, just for once?'

'But it was Susan I came to talk about.'

'I know. And I was half-expecting you to arrive, though perhaps not quite so quickly. I thought she'd send you along sooner or later.'

'Then why not tell me what it's all about?'

'Not on an empty stomach, anyway.'

'Later, then?'

He smiled, but there was no promise in his look.

'After all,' I said, 'it is a bit unfair on her to do this all of a sudden, and not even tell her why.'

'D'you know,' he said, 'I simply don't mind whether it's unfair or not. Isn't it odd? I simply don't mind.' He stood up. He was still half-smiling. 'I'm not sure that I'm not even taking a certain pleasure in the discovery that I'm

27

capable of being unfair to Susan—though that's in confidence, of course. I wouldn't tell everybody. After all, I have a reputation to keep up.'

'Then you're getting just a little bit tired of that reputation at last, are you?'

'Well, I wouldn't go so far as to say that.'

I finished my sherry and stood up beside him. 'We'll talk about it later,' I said. 'You haven't got rid of the subject. Have I been put in the usual room?'

'I imagine so.' He was going to ring for Mrs Fawcett but I stopped him.

'I know my way,' I said.

The room was on the first floor. When I went into it, I found Mrs Fawcett making up the bed. Going to the other side of it to help her, I asked her about her legs, which was one of the things one always did ask her, and she replied obliquely by saying, 'Oh, the food, Mrs Baynes, the food! What can one do about it with nothing in the shops?'

I should have liked to answer, 'Learn to cook what you can get.' But there was never much need to reply to Mrs Fawcett.

'It's the food, that's what it is,' she said. 'There's no nourishment in it, that's what's wrong. It doesn't do you any good. You eat, and your stomach feels full, and then what happens to it? I say to Mr Rice, "You can say what you like," I say, "but it's the food, that's what it is."'

'Then is there something wrong with Mr Rice?' I asked.

She pursed her lips and nodded her head, picking up a pillow to push it into a pillow-slip.

'It's like my last gentleman,' she said, 'Mr Daintree, whom I may have happened to mention. A very nice gentleman, well-educated and always considerate, though I haven't a good word to say for the rest of the family. Imposed on him, that's what they did. I used to tell him so. "They impose on you, Mr Daintree," I said, "it's only your money they're after." "Never mind, Mrs Fawcett," he used to say, "they'll be surprised when they see my will—and so will you, Mrs Fawcett. I haven't forgotten you in my will, Mrs Fawcett." Then he'd laugh, poor gentleman, just as if the pain weren't tearing his insides apart.'

I interrupted her. 'I don't understand. Are you trying to tell me that Mr Rice is ill?'

Her face lengthened mournfully, but apart from that she went on as if I had not spoken. 'A nice surprise it was too, Mrs Baynes, a very nice little surprise for me. He used to say to me, "I don't want you to want in your old age, Mrs Fawcett, after all you've done for me, and you the only one here who hasn't been after my money." A very good, kind, religious man he was. I always said it was the food done it, not the ulcers like they said. Terrible pain he suffered before he died, and always cheerful. The family tried to get rid of me near the end

29

because they knew I was the only real friend he had, but when the pain came on it was always me he wanted. "Make me some nice hot milk, Mrs Fawcett," he used to say—'

'Mrs Fawcett!' I snatched the sheet out of her hand so that she looked at me in surprise. 'What's wrong with Mr Rice? Has he got gastric ulcers or something? Is he really ill.'

'It's just the food,' she answered. 'Whatever they tell you, it's just the food.' Thinking, apparently, that my taking the sheet from her meant that I preferred to make the bed by myself, she pottered over to the dressing-table, unfolded a starched, embroidered cloth on it, murmured, 'I hope you've everything you want, Mrs Baynes,' and withdrew.

I looked round. I hated this room. It was a huge, haunted kind of place. But one almost wanted it to be haunted so that one might have a little company in its great, chilly spaces. One would have had to leave the electric-fire burning in it for three hours even to begin to warm it. Heavy pieces of mahogany stood about in it, like islands in a sullen sea. The paintwork was all of the shade of melting milk-chocolate, like that in the hall, and the curtains were dingy brown velvet.

When I had finished the bed, I sat down and dug into my bag for a pair of slippers. I was sitting there when someone tapped on the door, and when I answered, it was Beryl who came in. She stood there irresolutely, saying,

30

'Daddy told me you'd come,' and looking at me as if she were not quite convinced by the sight of me.

I told her to shut the door and stop the draught. She did so, but came only a step or two further into the room. I was still thinking about Norman's possible illness, and thought of asking her about it, but luckily I stopped myself in time. Norman was just the kind of man who would keep all information on such a subject from his children.

'That's a very nice dress you've got on,' I said, since she seemed to have nothing to say herself.

'Mummy bought it for me,' she said.

It was pale green, tight-waisted, full-skirted, and made her look so grown-up compared with my last memory of her, that I realised with a little shock that the child really was going to be quite as lovely as Susan. She had Susan's light gold hair and brown eyes. But she had an even better figure, and if anything, more delicate features.

'And she got my hair cut like this,' she said, putting her hand up self-consciously. 'D'you like it?'

'Very much.'

She fingered the folds of her skirt. 'Have you seen Mummy?'

'I saw her this morning.'

She seemed to have another question in her mind, yet not to want to ask it. I thought she

31

looked angry, although her voice was soft. But if it was not anger that was contracting her face, then she was intensely unhappy.

This surprised me, because Beryl had never struck me as being particularly fond of Susan. It had not occurred to me that even if Norman had told her that she was to see no more of her mother, she would be much upset.

Going to the dressing-table, I started combing my hair. Beryl watched me silently for a moment, then suddenly she turned on her heel and went out, purposely banging the door a little behind her. The bang meant that I had been right, she was angry. But with whom?

When I went downstairs again a few minutes later, I found Norman, Beryl and Maurice waiting for me in the drawing-room. Dinner was ready and we went through immediately to the panelled dining-room, and arranged ourselves round a half-acre of table. Maurice sat beside me. He was two years older than Beryl, a stolid, silent, un-get-atable boy, not very tall and of a heavy build, with upstanding, curly brown hair and severe grey eyes. I had always had an idea that if only one could get him to talk he would turn out to be likeable and intelligent, but at least in the presence of his family it was impossible to get him to make the first moves of human intercourse. I had not expected to find him there that evening, because he was studying zoology at the Imperial College, and it was term-time.

I said to him, 'Home for the week-end, Maurice?'

He nodded without speaking, and began on his boiled fish.

'D'you come home most week-ends?' I asked.

'Sometimes,' he said. His taciturnity was not offensive, but sounded merely as if he could imagine no possible reason for saying more.

'It's the first time since the term started,' said Beryl, putting some meaning into the remark that I did not grasp, but which Maurice did, because he answered it with a slight shrug of his shoulders.

'I believe we've had boiled fish rather recently, haven't we?' Norman remarked vaguely, looking unenthusiastically at his plate.

'Yesterday,' said Beryl.

'Poor Mrs Fawcett isn't very imaginative,' said Norman, 'and there are so many things nowadays I'm not supposed to eat. Perhaps unfortunately, boiled fish isn't one of them.'

If this was Mrs Fawcett's usual way of boiling fish, I should have said the misfortune was a serious one. The fish was wet and crumbling, with bones protruding at all points and with an ambitious flavouring of half-cooked onion. The potatoes were flannel-grey and there were some mushy, boiled, dried peas.

'Are you on a diet?' I asked Norman.

'Well, of a sort,' he said. 'It's some damn-fool idea of Dr Snow's, and I'm letting him try it out on me for the sake of peace. I know there's nothing the matter with me, it's only nerves. I know my nerves. They're treacherous, troublesome things, but they're mine and I know how to handle them.'

'Where's John?' Beryl interrupted him abruptly.

It might have been a clumsy attempt to come to his help, because she knew he disliked talking about his health, or it might have been the seizing of a chance to show that she did not care about it and did not mean to let him enjoy having my attention upon it. I thought that that was how Norman understood her interruption, for he gave her a curious resigned look, as if he found this attitude in her uncomfortable for himself but entirely natural.

I explained about John being in Holland. Then, through a simple association of ideas, remembering how I had meant to use John's absence, I said suddenly, 'Norman, aren't you ever going to do anything about this house?'

He looked surprised. 'What should I do about it?'

'Well, covering up a little of this dusky paint with something a bit brighter would help to make it less grotesque and detestable,' I said. 'But selling the place and buying something quite, quite different would really be best.'

'Sounds like much too much of an upheaval at my time of life,' he said. 'And I don't think

Beryl or Maurice particularly want to move. Do you?' he questioned them.

Maurice shrugged again and Beryl gave a laugh. Without looking at her father, she said, 'I couldn't move from the district, because I've just started being trained as a market-gardener. It's a new idea. I only began last week. I used to think I wanted to be a dressmaker, but now I'm going to be a gardener instead. Would you ever have believed it?'

Again, from a deliberately false sound in her voice, I knew she was saying something to her father and brother that she was not saying to me, but it was beyond me to guess what it was.

Maurice scowled and said, 'Shut up.'

Norman said mildly, 'Redecoration would be enormously expensive just now, I imagine.'

It went on like that right through dinner, with Beryl dropping hints about something which she had not quite the courage to let me understand, and Norman incompetently trying to change the subject, while Maurice grew steadily sulkier and more uncomfortable. After dinner he seemed glad to be sent over to the Weinkrauts to fetch my bag.

Ernst came back with him and had coffee with us. At first I was pleased, because his presence covered up for the time being some of the family tension. But presently Maurice said that he must go upstairs and do some work and went out, and soon afterwards Beryl said that

35

she must go to bed, since she had to get up very early, now that she was learning to be a gardener. After that I should have been glad if Ernst had gone, because I could have settled down to the talk I must sooner or later have with Norman.

But Ernst stayed. I did not think he had any particular object in staying, except that he was in the habit of coming over like this and talking to Norman until his own bedtime. It was about eleven o'clock when he left.

Norman, by then, was looking very tired. The shadows from the lamp, as he changed his chair after Ernst had gone and sat down nearer the fire, made his face seem startlingly drawn and exhausted. I had never seen it look like that.

I said dubiously, 'I suppose I oughtn't to try and make you talk now, you're looking terrible. What's the matter, Norman?'

He replied only to the first part of my remark. 'What d'you want to talk about, Marabelle?'

'You know,' I said. 'But what's wrong with you, Norman? You aren't well, are you?'

'Oh, there's nothing much wrong that old age can't explain,' he answered casually.

'You aren't old,' I said.

'Old enough, thanks. As I said, it's just nerves. I've got worries, like most people, and mine always hit my insides. Stupid, but there it is.'

'About these worries ...'

He gave a sigh. 'I really am rather tired.'

'And don't want to talk—I know. But Norman—'

'Yes?'

'Please tell me why you suddenly won't let Susan into your house, then I can go away to-morrow and not bother you any more?'

'But why go away to-morrow, Marabelle? We love having you here.'

'Oh dear, Norman, you're a twisty creature, aren't you?'

He smiled. 'Perhaps.'

'You see,' I went on, 'it's only the inconsistency that's upsetting. If you'd refused to see Susan from the moment she left you, I and everybody else would have thought it the most natural thing in the world. But for ten years you let her come here whenever she wanted to. You let her go on arranging your life, engaging your housekeepers for you, almost running your home at a distance. And then suddenly you stop it. You stop it and won't say why. Well, that's worrying. And you aren't well, and perhaps the two things have something to do with each other, and that's worrying too—'

'They've got nothing whatever to do with each other, Marabelle. Thanks all the same for caring.'

I looked at him doubtfully. 'Is that honest?'

'Yes. Really.'

37

'Not heroics?'

'I didn't know I was supposed to have the kind of character that went in for them.'

'But then—'

He leant forward, resting his elbows on the arm of his chair. 'Marabelle, it sounds to me as if you've got quite a mistaken idea of me. When Susan left me, I had one simple reason for letting her go on coming here as much as she liked. I should think you're intelligent enough to be able to think out for yourself what it was without my having to talk about it. I'd rather not talk about it. I'd rather not talk about any of it. I may have been wrong all along, but if so, I couldn't help it. I did what seemed best ... But something in the situation changed, and so I had to change—'

There was a tap on the door. Norman said, 'Come in,' and Mrs Fawcett came in, carrying a small, silver tray with a mug on it.

'Here's your milk, Mr Rice,' she said, 'and as soon as you've drunk it off you go to bed. No sitting up talking till all hours.' She put the tray down beside him. 'You'll see to that, won't you, Mrs Baynes? When he's drunk his milk, he's to go straight off to bed.'

Norman said, 'Thank you, Mrs Fawcett— yes, I'll be good.' As she went out, he added, 'She's an old dear, isn't she? She reminds me of a nurse I used to have. What was I saying?'

'Oh well, perhaps we ought not to talk about it any longer,' I said. 'I expect Mrs Fawcett's

38

quite right, you ought to be in bed.'

He sipped the hot milk, looking as if he enjoyed it. 'Didn't I tell you old age was coming on? Second childhood, so to speak. But about Susan ... You know, I've never particularly blamed her for anything. There've been times when I've hated her like the devil, but I've never blamed her much.'

'It rather surprises me to hear you're capable of hating any one,' I said.

'Dear me, you do seem to have an odd idea of me,' he said. 'Yes, certainly I can hate ... But I don't like doing it, you know. It's an uncomfortable feeling.' He drank the rest of the milk and set the mug down on the tray. 'Sometimes I think I may always have been unduly attached to my comfort. A little bit of hating now and then does seem to increase one's sense of responsibility. But it's not a nice feeling.'

'Go along to bed,' I said. 'We'll talk to-morrow.'

He stood up. 'Are you staying up?'

'For a bit. I'm not sleepy.'

'Well, good night, then.'

When he had gone I sat still for a while, looking into the fire, thinking about Norman and about Maurice and Beryl, and about all the undercurrents in their talk. Norman had nearly told me something several times, and then had changed his mind. I had a feeling that he would have liked to talk, but for some reason had made up his mind that he must not.

Suddenly I remembered Susan's saying that she would write to me, and wondered again why she had thought it necessary. But I knew that she had a very purposive mind. She seldom did anything without some curious but considered motive.

I thought it was obvious that Norman's decision to keep her away from the house had something to do with the children, probably with Beryl in particular. He must have decided that Susan's influence had become harmful to the girl. But I did not think that a new haircut and some pretty, grown-up clothes would have had that effect on him. Norman always noticed and liked pretty clothes, and since her infancy had taken pride in Beryl's charm. It occurred to me that he might suddenly have become afraid that he would soon lose her, and so had become resentful of her beauty. But he had never tried to stop her going about with young men, or looked too closely into how she spent her time with them.

I got up, thinking that after all I might as well go to bed, and switched off the light.

As I did so, a new thought came into my mind, and I went back to the fire, standing in front of it, enjoying its heat, and liking the change in the room when it was lit only by the red glow from the hearth. The new thought had nothing to do with Norman or Susan. It was simply a glowing vision of how my own sitting-room would look when I had painted its walls.

I like thinking about that sort of thing so much better than about other people's problems that after a moment I sat down again, lit another cigarette and went on adding details to the vision. When a drowsiness crept up on me, I thought vaguely of bed, but at the same time thought what a pity it would be to waste the fire. I suppose I sat there for about half an hour. But perhaps it was longer.

The whole house was quiet, full of the sense of sleep and deep night-time that could never have come in London till many hours later. Perhaps I dozed. But I know that when I heard a sound behind me, I instantly started upright in my chair, feeling that this meant trouble, that no one could be moving about at that hour on lawful business.

This was not really surprising considering that the sound that I had heard was that of somebody climbing in at the window.

CHAPTER FOUR

I have never had the least doubt as to how I should behave if I met a burglar. I should simply keep very still and hope that he would assume that I was asleep or dead.

Now, without one second's hesitation, I adopted this course of action. I even had the presence of mind to throw the remains of my cigarette into the fire, for neither a corpse nor a Sleeping Beauty should have a half-smoked cigarette in one hand. Though for the moment I kept my eyes half-open, I was ready to close them convincingly at the first necessity. I was horribly frightened.

The burglar was rather clumsy. He hurt himself getting in at the window and swore peevishly. Then he went on talking to himself, which, in the circumstances, I thought imprudent. He was still talking to himself, and rubbing one of his shins, when he fumbled his way through the heavy, velvet curtains.

He had on a long dark overcoat and a felt hat, he had a small bag in one hand and held a torch in the other. The torch was on but he seemed much more concerned with the damage to himself than with looking round the room. Putting the torch down on the floor, so that its beam lit only a strip of carpet, he pulled up one trouser leg and very tenderly felt round the area of the bruise or the wound, whichever it was. Sounding only half-convinced but anxious to console himself, he muttered, 'Nothing serious,' then picked up the torch again and began to advance cautiously across the room.

By that time I had recovered myself. I said, 'Do shut the window behind you, Sholto—there's a horrible draught.'

He jumped as if I had hit him, swung the

torch round on to me, stared at me with as much horror as if I were in fact the corpse I had thought of representing, then let out a shaky breath.

'That wasn't nice of you,' he said. 'It wasn't at all nice. Really it was rather cruel. You startled me horribly.'

'You startled me,' I said.

He did not trouble to consider that. 'I never imagined there'd be any one here,' he said. 'You really shouldn't have spoken suddenly like that. It gave me a nasty shock.'

'Poor Sholto—I'm so sorry,' I said. 'But you might still shut the window.'

He went back to the window, limping a little, and shut it.

'You've hurt yourself,' I said.

'It's nothing,' he said bravely. 'Nothing much. But what on earth are you doing here?'

'What are *you* doing here, Sholto?'

'Oh, I—I happened to be in the neighbourhood.'

'Can't you do better than that?'

He gave a grin. 'Perhaps—when I've thought about it.' He came back to the fire and dropped into a chair. I reached out for the switch of a table-lamp and tilted the shade so that the light shone on to him. Blinking, he dropped his hat on the floor beside him and pushed his fingers through his close-cut, curly hair.

I had always thought that Sholto Dapple,

43

Susan's second husband, had the look of a conjurer, of being ready at almost any moment to pull cards out of his sleeves or eggs out of his ears. It was something to do with the shape of his long, horselike face and his mild, mysterious, deceptively confiding manner. In fact he was a lecturer at the London School of Psychology and Visual Education, or a place with some such name. He was ten years younger than Susan. His marriage to her had survived in full being for about six months and taken about another eighteen to slide through the various stages of dissolution to divorce. By the time that had come about he was living with his mother once more, deeply thankful, I had always felt sure, to have been cured of marriage, and so grateful to Susan for having achieved this for him that he had been delighted to go on running little errands for her and occasionally taking her out to dinner.

Taking a silk handkerchief out of his pocket, he wiped his forehead, doing it with the style which made me expect to see a hen come flapping out of the handkerchief.

'So she sent you along too, did she?' he said. 'When did you get here?'

'About dinner-time,' I said. 'I came on the fourteen.'

'So did I,' said Sholto. 'Funny I didn't see you. I had dinner at the pub.'

'Seems to have been a long dinner.'

'Well, I had a drink or two with some

44

cheerful characters after it. Then, of course, I had to wait till things got quiet around here. I've been walking past the house at intervals for the last hour, waiting for all the lights to go out.'

'I don't understand the manoeuvre,' I said. 'Why not simply walk up to the front door at a reasonable hour and ring the bell?'

'Is that what you did?'

'Of course.'

'Cunning,' said Sholto. 'I never thought of it.'

'Why? Did you expect to be forcibly thrown out?'

'Not exactly—but I'd have had to think up a reason for my coming, shouldn't I? What reason did you give Norman?'

'The real one,' I said. 'Why not? It's a natural enough thing to want to know, isn't it?'

'Yes, but it's warning him, isn't it? He'd never give you an answer you could trust.'

I frowned, feeling bogged. The conversation did not seem to me to be making sense. 'I fail to see how breaking into his house in the middle of the night is going to help you to find out from Norman why he's suddenly decided to stop Susan coming here and seeing the children.'

Sholto's eyebrows arched sharply and he gave me a hard stare.

A moment later he was annoyed with himself for having given himself away to that

45

extent, and he passed a hand over his face, wiping out all expression but a vague smile.

'No,' he said, 'come to think of it, when you put it like that, I don't either. Stupid of me. I'm a fool. Where's John, by the way.'

I yawned. I knew we had been at cross-purposes but I was too sleepy to bother to clear it up. 'In Bermuda,' I said.

'In Bermuda—really? He flew, I suppose. I saw him in Kingsway only last week. What's he doing?'

'He's gone there with a half-negro woman.'

'No!' Sholto's eyebrows shot up again. It was what happened to them whenever he suffered some small surprise. 'Well, I'd never have thought it. I always thought that you and John ... But it just shows, doesn't it? I mean to say, one can know people, as one thinks, quite intimately, and yet not have the faintest idea of what they're likely to do next?'

'Yes,' I said, 'it just shows.'

'Do you—do you mind much, Marabelle?'

'Terribly,' I said. 'Now for God's sake, let's go to bed. I'd better find you a room, I suppose.'

'Oh, don't bother,' he said, 'I can manage anywhere. I dare say I shan't stay.'

'You'd better stay till breakfast anyway, and tell Norman what you're doing here,' I said.

'But with you here for the same reason, that's hardly necessary. I can easily slip back to the pub.'

'It's obvious we aren't here for the same reason—unless I don't know the real reason why I'm here, which is beginning to seem to me more than possible.' I got up.

Sholto remained seated. 'I don't know what you're talking about. But this woman, Marabelle—'

'She's as beautiful as the Queen of Sheba and she has six children. Come along. I can't promise you sheets or pyjamas, but I know where there's a room with a bed in it.'

'Can't we stay and talk a bit?' said Sholto. 'I'd like to know how John met her. I never seem to meet any women.'

'Because you don't want to,' I said.

'But I do, I do! Oh, do sit down and talk. There are all sorts of things about myself that I'd like to discuss with you.'

'To-morrow,' I said.

He stood up reluctantly. 'Oh well, show me this room.'

It was a small room at the top of the stairs. There was a bed in it with some blankets, and Sholto said in a discouraged tone that it would do. He was not very quiet about it and as I half-expected, the noise he made brought both Maurice and Beryl out of their rooms. Neither of them showed much surprise at seeing Sholto, and Maurice produced some pyjamas and Beryl some sheets, so that in the end Sholto was fairly comfortable.

Beryl followed me to my room. She looked

47

nearly asleep, rosy and beautiful.

Standing in the doorway, she whispered, 'I've got to get up very early in the morning, so I expect I shan't see you then. You'll still be here when I get back, won't you?'

'I don't expect so,' I said. 'I think I'll be going home in the morning.'

'I wish you'd stay,' she said. 'I've been thinking things over and I'd rather like your advice about something. Couldn't you stay?'

'Well, perhaps. But I meant to go home in the morning.'

'Do stay, please. Incidentally, I think Sholto's mad, don't you?'

'No madder than most people.'

'I think Mummy drove him mad.' She turned and went back to her room.

Making up my mind not to think about anything that had happened that day, I undressed as quickly as I could and got into bed.

I was successful in not thinking much and soon fell asleep. But my dreams took revenge on me for this, giving me back the events of the evening with an insane twist. For instance, Mrs Fawcett had become a negress and Norman introduced her to me as the Queen of Hearts. The odd thing was that she was not black, nor did she look any different from when I had last seen her, yet, as happens in dreams, it was self-evident that she was a negress. Then a man in a top hat and a black cloak appeared and said, 'Have you any pilchards? I like pilchards?' and I became anxious in the extreme that he might discover a tin of pilchards that I kept in a black hatbox, and which I had kept there for years to celebrate the end of the war. Somebody said to me, 'That war's over,' and I said, 'But I heard a siren in Kingsway only last week . . .' And so on. It was all far more upsetting than it sounds, and I was glad to wake up.

I did not know what time it was, but I had the feeling that I had not been asleep long. Settling myself to try to sleep again, I was just drifting off when I was jerked into complete wakefulness by a noise in the passage. Perhaps it was a similar noise that had wakened me in the first place.

It was a very soft noise, so soft as to be thoroughly suspicious. Sitting up, I listened. The house and the garden and the world beyond it were wrapped in silence, all except this faint, sinister, sliding sound in the passage.

I got out of bed, and tiptoeing to the door, I opened it a crack, ready to slam it shut again and yell my head off if I saw anything frightening. It was only Sholto. He was creeping very carefully along the passage, his torch in his hand.

I said, 'Whatever do you think you're doing?' and switched on the passage light.

He jumped as he had when I spoke to him in the drawing-room, turned, saw me and

49

frowned in exasperation.

'Please don't do that, Marabelle!' he said in a high, peevish tone. 'It's cruel to jump out on a person suddenly like that. I believe you've got a thoroughly sadistic streak in you.'

'I'm sure I have,' I said. 'All the same, just what are you doing?'

'What should I be doing?' he said. 'Looking for the bathroom, of course.'

'The bathroom, as you so politely call it, is in the other direction.'

'Is it? Oh, thanks.'

'And you've been in this house quite often enough to know it.'

'I haven't been here for ages.'

'Well, now you know.'

'Yes. Thank you, Marabelle. I'm sorry I disturbed you.'

'I hope you won't do it again.' Shutting the door I went back to bed.

I heard him go down the passage to his own room, but I left my light on so that, in case he wanted to play any more tricks, he should know I was still listening. There was something I had not much liked about seeing him creeping down the passage like that, with something in his hand which, although he had hidden it behind him the moment he turned and saw me, I was sure had been a jemmy.

CHAPTER FIVE

I fell asleep again without turning off the light, and again slept restlessly, dreaming too much. When I awoke, the time was half past seven. I do not often wake so early.

As I lay there, I heard a door bang, then footsteps below my window, together with what sounded like a bicycle being wheeled over the gravel. I supposed that it was Beryl, starting out on her day's work. I tried to go to sleep again.

A quarter of an hour later, finding myself more wide-awake than before, I got up. I had just had an idea. If I were to go down to the kitchen, I could make some drinkable coffee and some toast and bring it all back to bed, thus escaping the breakfast that Mrs Fawcett was likely to inflict on me. If I could also find a book, I should be able to stay here quietly and comfortably for as long as I felt inclined.

I went downstairs. The morning was cool and the big silent house gave one the feeling that it would take hours to warm up. But the sky was blue and there was a pale, bright sparkle in the air. The leaves were not gone from the trees yet, though the russet of the beeches in the garden was past its best, and the lawn was scattered with damp, yellow leaves.

As I went into the kitchen, I saw the

milkman go past the window. I heard the clink of the bottles as he put them down on the step outside the door, and heard him whistling as he went away again. He took the path across the garden towards the Weinkrauts' bungalow, pushing his way through the hedge and crossing their lawn to reach their back door.

I put the kettle on the stove and hunted around the kitchen for cups and saucers, coffee, and the other things I wanted. The kitchen was full of odds and ends belonging to Mrs Fawcett's private life. There was a work-basket on the window-sill, bulging with tangled tape-measures and coloured wools. There were some photographs on the mantelpiece, all of them of elderly gentlemen with stiff collars. One of them, I supposed, was Mr Fawcett, and I settled on one who was even more of a picture of death-in-life than the others as best fitting the part. Then it occurred to me that I had never once heard her speak of her husband. I had heard of a father and brothers and nephews, and of several employers, but not of one single husband. That was odd, when one came to think of it.

I was at the stove, making some toast, when I heard a light tap on the window. I had not heard any one approach, so when I turned and saw a man's face pressed against the glass, I was startled. But it was only Ernst Weinkraut.

He gestured to me to open the window. I did so and he laid a single rose on the sill. It was deep red and wonderfully scented.

'For you,' he said, 'because I love you so much.'

'Why, that's very nice of you, Ernst,' I said. 'But how on earth d'you produce things like this at this time of year?'

'By love,' he said. 'Love can achieve anything.'

'I might agree with you later in the day, but it's too early for me to have fine thoughts like that,' I said. 'Are you off to work already?'

He nodded. 'Tell me, how are things here? No trouble, like you feared.'

'Well, I'm not sure,' I said. 'Things are a bit peculiar.'

'Yes—but it is, after all, a peculiar household. I shouldn't worry. You come over and see us again later, no?'

'I'm not quite sure how long I'm staying,' I said. 'Be a dear and pass me those milk bottles, will you?'

Ernst stooped to pick the bottles off the step and handed them in at the window. There were three pint bottles. Two had aluminium caps, the third was shiny gilt. Ernst tapped the yellow top. 'That is Norman's—T.T. It goes in the refrigerator.'

'You seem to know the ways of the house pretty well,' I said.

'Vy not? I like to know about people. Now, Marabelle—' He leant his elbows on the outer sill. 'I ask you something. You think it over and

53

tell me later vot you think. It is important.'

At that moment I became aware that I had been smelling burning for about the last minute. It was the toast, kindled into a small fire under the grill. Removing the remains, I shovelled them regretfully into the sink-basket and cut another two slices of bread.

'Marabelle—' said Ernst.

'Go ahead,' I said.

'But please listen carefully. This is important to me. Do you think I should change my name to Vinnicott?'

'No,' I said.

'You don't like it? Vincott, then? It is simpler.'

'No.'

'Vinkle?'

'I like it best the way it is,' I said.

'But think, Marabelle—please think. To have a wife who cannot pronounce her own name properly, to listen to that every day of one's life ... You don't think it would be better to change it?'

'No.'

He scratched his head. 'I thought you would like Vinnicott. But you think it over, no?'

'All right,' I said. 'And thank you very much for the rose.'

He smiled and walked off. I nursed the second two slices of toast carefully, made the coffee, put the T.T. milk in the refrigerator and heated a little out of one of the other bottles,

54

which I left on the kitchen table, put everything on a tray and then started hunting in a cupboard for some sort of glass worthy of Ernst's rose. I was just arranging it in a little vase I had found, when a figure went rapidly by outside the window, a key was pushed into the latch of the back door, the door was opened and a young man I had never seen before walked in, saw me, smiled happily and said, 'I'm Basil.'

It would have felt natural to reply, 'I'm Marabelle,' but in the moment that I hesitated, he walked smartly across the kitchen, disappeared into the scullery, closed the door behind him and called through it, 'Please don't come in for a moment. I'm changing my trousers.'

I sat down in the nearest chair and thought about it.

I had not been warned in any way. I had heard nobody mention any Basil. For all I knew, I ought to have rushed straight for the police.

The modern burglar, after all, often goes to work in broad daylight and with an air of confidence. He comes prepared to read gas meters, mend sash cords and do other useful things. Perhaps he likes to change his trousers before he gets down to the job. This young man had been wearing a smart, checked tweed jacket and one of the cleanest pairs of flannel trousers that I have ever seen. I also had an impression that he had been wearing grey suede shoes, a pale primrose shirt and a pullover in the colours of autumn leaves. He had been carrying a small leather bag. This might have contained a spare pair of trousers, but it might just as well be meant for removing the swag.

While I thought about it I had a cup of coffee. After about three minutes the young man reappeared. He had changed into a pair of corduroys, an old pair of tennis shoes, and had discarded the tweed coat.

'Have some coffee,' I said uncertainly.

'Oh, that's awfully nice of you,' he said. 'I'd love some.'

'Milk and sugar?'

'Please.'

He looked about twenty-five, was not very tall, was built with extreme neatness and grace, and had curly golden hair and blue eyes. It was a little difficult to believe in him.

I fetched a second cup and poured out some coffee for him.

'It's a nice morning,' I said.

'Yes, isn't it?' he said, beaming. 'I feel wonderful to-day.'

'I'm glad,' I murmured.

'That's a beautiful rose,' he went on. 'I adore roses.'

'I like them too,' I said.

'They're my favourite flower, I think. But I haven't any in my garden. They're so expensive

56

to buy now, you know, and I'm saving up to buy myself some tails.'

'I can imagine you in tails better than in a garden,' I said.

'Oh, I've only a teeny-tiny patch. I work it with a trowel.'

'I've a window-box at home,' I said. 'I dig that with a pencil.'

'I often think about window-boxes,' he said, gravely, pleased to find we had something in common. 'Where d'you live?'

'London,' I replied.

'London! That's where I'd like to live. But d'you know what I'd like most of all?'

'No,' I said.

'I'd like to go abroad.'

'Anywhere in particular?'

'No, just abroad—somewhere different from here. But I don't suppose I ever shall.'

'Why not?'

'Because I never do anything I want to. I'm like that.' He put his cup down. 'Thanks ever so much for the coffee.' He disappeared into the scullery again.

From the noise he made there I thought he must be routing about inside a cupboard, and after a moment he reappeared carrying a bucket, some firewood and some old newspapers.

'I generally do the fires first,' he said as if he were asking for my approval.

'That sounds all right,' I said.

57

'Then I do the dining-room and get on with the lounge while they're at breakfast.'

'Go right ahead,' I said. 'It's nothing to do with me.'

He paused, looking at me thoughtfully. 'Then you aren't the new housekeeper?'

I shook my head. 'Why—is there going to be a new housekeeper?'

'Not that I know of.'

'Then why did you think that's who I was?'

'Because it would have been so nice if you were. Oh, I wish you were!' He gave a brave smile to hide the extent of his disappointment, and went out.

I had got it straight by now. Basil was the charwoman. It was the result of his dusting and polishing that had so impressed me in the hall the evening before.

It seemed rather late in the day to take my breakfast upstairs, so I went on with it in the kitchen. In a minute Basil was back. He had a letter in his hand.

'Post's just come,' he said. 'Are you Mrs Baynes?'

'Yes.'

He handed me the letter and went out again.

It was the letter from Susan. She has one of those enormous handwritings that cover a whole envelope with an address. As soon as I saw it, I felt a sharp misgiving. It was quite unlikely that she would have bothered to write simply to thank me for having come here on her errand.

The letter ran, 'Marabelle dear, bless you for being an angel. I knew I could count on you. I'm writing just to tell you how everlastingly grateful I feel and—' That was the bottom of the first page. I turned it over and went on. '—I'll do anything on earth to make it up to you. By the way, while you're down there, you might just look around and see if you can see my Roger Clegg anywhere. It's been missing ever since Norman was here. I rather think he may have it. With eternal love and gratitude, Susan.'

I crumpled the letter up violently, threw it into a corner of the kitchen and swore. So that was it. The Roger Clegg.

Even so, there was a great deal about the situation that I could not understand. I knew the Clegg was one of Susan's most prized possessions, mostly, I had always thought, from snobbishness, because I did not believe that on its own merits, Susan had ever cared for one picture more than another. But still, particularly since Clegg started coming back into fashion, she had paraded her ownership, and had once refused an offer for the picture of a hundred and fifty pounds. I had never cared for it much myself. It was of some women picnicking in a meadow, a dim, rather genteel affair. The special thing about it was that our grandmother was one of the women, and Clegg had made a present to her of the picture. She, in her turn, had given it to our mother, and she had given it to Susan.

Lighting a cigarette, I tried to think. Susan implied that Norman had come to visit her, had not found her in and had walked off with the Clegg.

It sounded fantastic. But it was possible to this extent, that Norman had always adored the picture, and when he and Susan separated he had done his best to persuade her to let him keep it. He had offered to buy it or to let her have all sorts of things in exchange, but she had refused even to consider being parted from it.

But still, I thought, would Norman simply steal a picture?

No. But he might not have considered it stealing. He might have decided that Susan owed him something in return for all his forbearance. If so, I agreed with him, and saw no reason for helping Susan in getting the picture back. In any case, he valued it far more genuinely than she did.

I understood Sholto's presence now, and his odd behaviour. Susan must have seen him after she had seen me, and realising that my reaction to the discovery of what she really wanted might not be advantageous to her, she had persuaded him to come down here and try a little plain burglary. Presumably she believed that Norman had refused her admittance to the house in case she should find the picture herself.

60

I was thinking over all these things when Basil came back. He was carrying a bucketful of ashes and was on his way to the dust-bin with them when I stopped him. Since I had decided not to help Susan, I do not quite know why I spoke as I did. 'Basil, you clean this whole house, don't you?' I said.

'Most of it,' he said, 'though of course I can't keep all of it equally clean—there isn't time. Some of it, like the lounge and the dining-room, I do every day, and I generally get round the rest of it during the week, but I can't really help it if some of the paintwork and the brass isn't quite what I'd like it to be, because—'

'That isn't what I meant,' I said. 'I meant, you do go over the whole house, don't you? You go into all the different rooms.'

'All but the study,' he said.

'You don't go into the study?'

'No—not now.' He blushed slightly, as if he were embarrassed.

'Why not?' I asked.

'Well, you see, I used to put things straight in there.'

'What things?'

'Well, I used to tidy up.'

'What was wrong with that?'

'I don't know,' he said helplessly. 'I only used to put the books back on the shelves and arrange the papers in piles. Mr Rice didn't like it. He told me not to. But I—I went on doing it.'

'Oh,' I said. 'Why did you do that?'

61

'I couldn't help it. I'm like that.'

'Oh, I see. So now you aren't allowed into the study?'

He nodded, still with burning cheeks, as if I had made him confess something disgraceful.

'And how long has this been going on?' I asked.

'Since the beginning of last week.'

So the picture, if it was in the house at all, was obviously in Norman's study.

However, to make sure, I went on, 'I suppose you don't happen to have noticed a new picture anywhere in the house during the last few days?'

He thought it over carefully before he answered. He did not seem at all curious about why I was asking him these questions. 'What kind of a picture?'

'A rather small one, about eighteen inches by twenty-four, of several women in bustles, having a picnic in a meadow.'

'No,' he said. 'But then, I haven't been looking out for it. But I'll start looking now, if you like.'

'Don't you think you'd have noticed it, if it had been there?'

'Well, I might or I might not, depending on what I was thinking about at the time, and on how high up it was hung, and so on. If I'd had to dust it, for instance, I'd have noticed it, or if I was looking upwards for cobwebs, but if I was just going round in the usual way and thinking

62

hard about something else, it's quite likely I shouldn't have noticed anything unusual.'

'I wonder what you think about, Basil,' I said, 'when you're thinking hard.'

He shifted from one foot to the other. 'Well, I tell myself things sometimes, like what I'm going to do when I get home in the evening. Or I think about railway trains and ships. I'm always rather sick when I go in them, and I think that by thinking about them enough perhaps I could cure myself.'

'Good luck to you,' I said. 'And you don't think you've noticed a picture?'

'I'm afraid not. I'm ever so sorry.'

'Don't let it trouble you.' I waited until he had gone out by the back door to take the ashes to the bin, then I got up and went into the hall.

Norman's study was a small room next to the dining-room. As long as I had known him, Norman had spent several hours a day in his study, writing a book on his philosophy of life. He had an odd theory about writing, characteristic of his modest attitude to most things. He believed that everything which it was possible to say had already been said by somebody else far better than it was possible for himself to say it. What followed, therefore, was that in writing a book, his job was only to stick together these things that had already been said into a new whole, the work becoming simply a gigantic job of scissors and paste. I quite understood his determination to keep out of the room any one likely to disarrange all his carefully collected and hoarded snippets.

As I went towards the study, I heard someone on the staircase above me. I did not particularly want to be seen spying in Norman's study, particularly by Norman himself, but I thought I had just time for a quick look round before the person, whoever it was, came into view. I grasped the handle.

The door would not budge. It was locked.

CHAPTER SIX

It was Mrs Fawcett on the stairs. She came down slowly, leaning heavily on the banisters. She was in her usual bunchy black dress and had a pale pink cardigan wrapped round her shoulders.

'Good morning, Mrs Baynes,' she said when she saw me, 'I hope you slept well. I never like that room you had myself. I shouldn't fancy sleeping in it by myself. It makes me think of things. Perhaps it reminds me of the room poor Mr Godstowe died in. It was about the same size, and at the end of a passage like that. I remember going along that passage every night to take him his hot drink—I remember it as if it was yesterday. He used to look up when he saw me and say, "Mrs Fawcett, I don't know what I'd do without my hot drink at night. You

64

certainly do know how to look after a man, Mrs Fawcett," he said.'

I was still thinking about the locked door of the study, but she seemed to expect me to say something. 'But he died, in spite of the hot drinks?' I said.

'Yes, poor man. I went in there one evening and his eyes was just staring at me fixed-like from the bed.'

'I'm not sure if I remember Mr Godstowe,' I said.

'He was my last but one. After him came Mr Daintree. It was the food that killed Mr Daintree. I always said—'

'And did Mr Godstowe leave you any money?'

'Well, it's funny you should ask that, because as a matter of fact, he did leave me a small sum. A very good, kind man, he was. But talking of food, Mrs Baynes, I haven't the faintest idea what I'm going to give you for breakfast. If you'd come yesterday there'd have been a nice little bit of haddock—'

'Don't worry about me, I've had breakfast,' I said and escaped into the dining-room, where Basil's fire was burning up cheeringly.

The first down to breakfast was Maurice. He ate fast, explaining he had a train to catch.

'Back to London?' I asked.

He nodded, of course avoiding the uttering of any unnecessary word.

'I suppose you won't be coming back this

65

evening?' I went on.

'Don't think so,' he said. 'Might come back at the week-end. Depends.'

'On what?'

'Dad, mostly.'

'D'you mean on how he is?'

'No, I didn't mean that. Why? D'you think there's anything much the matter with him?' He was looking at his plate, attacking a shrivelled kipper with concentration. I could not tell whether or not there was concern in his gruff voice.

'I can't make out,' I said.

'He says he's just a bit run down,' said Maurice. 'I think that's all it is. I think he'd tell me if it was anything else.'

'He generally takes you into his confidence, does he?'

'More or less.'

'This business about Susan, for instance—?'

He raised his head. His eyes were troubled. 'He's said nothing about that. He hasn't said anything about not wanting me to see her in London. He's only said he won't have her here.'

'Without explanations?'

'Absolutely without. That's why Beryl asked me to come down. She's awfully upset about it.'

'I never realised she was so fond of Susan,' I said.

'Nor did I. It's rather rum.'

'Yes, certainly it's rum.'

He left in a hurry a few minutes later.

I was considering going upstairs to get dressed, although usually I like to sit about reading newspapers and smoking until a good deal later in the morning, when Sholto appeared.

I had forgotten about Sholto for the moment, and seeing his long, horse's face slide tentatively round the edge of the door when I had been expecting Norman gave me a surprise. No place had been laid for Sholto, since no one had yet thought of mentioning his presence to Mrs Fawcett, but he came in and settled himself comfortably in what was obviously Norman's place.

'No Norman?' he said, helping himself to Norman's kipper. 'I thought he was an early riser.'

'I think he's taking life a bit easily at present,' I said. 'He's not very well.'

'No? I'm awfully sorry to hear that. I've always liked Norman. Naturally I have a lot of guilt-feelings towards him, but I do my best to forget that and to recognise that I really like him very much indeed.'

'Nice of you, Sholto,' I said.

He considered this, as he always did any remark about himself, seriously.

'Not really,' he said fairly. 'I think every one should try to be like that. We shouldn't let aggressive attitudes develop out of our guilt-

67

feelings. It isn't right.'

'Are these guilt-feelings due to having stolen his wife or to trying to steal his picture?' I asked.

'Ah, so you've got on to the picture,' he said. 'Why did you pretend last night you knew nothing about it?'

'I didn't know anything about it last night,' I said, 'but this morning I've had a letter from Susan that makes everything clear.'

'Well, I'm glad,' he said, 'because now we can get together. Would you like my advice?'

'I'd listen to it, anyway.'

'Then forget about it all. Leave the whole thing to me.'

'What, say nothing about it to Norman?'

'Of course say nothing to Norman! Your coming has probably done enough harm already. He's probably got the thing hidden away somewhere we'll never find it. I've been round most of the house and I haven't seen it.'

'Have you looked in his study?'

'No, it's locked.'

'Couldn't you have solved that little difficulty with your jemmy? I thought that's what they're for.'

'So did I,' he said, 'but the fact is, I don't really know how to use it without smashing the door to bits, and I thought Norman might be rather annoyed if I did that.'

'You don't think he'll be annoyed if you take the picture?'

'That's different. It isn't his. If it simply disappears, I don't think he'll even mention the fact.'

'I suppose,' I said thoughtfully, 'there isn't any doubt that he's got it.'

Sholto helped himself to more tea, thought for a moment and then said, 'It's impossible to be certain about another person, or oneself, for that matter, but my estimate of the situation is, he's got it. After all, he went to Susan's flat, apparently he was alone in the room with the picture for some time, and then the picture was missing. And he's always been mad about it and somehow resented the fact that Susan wouldn't let him have it. There's a lot more resentment in Norman than appears on the surface. I realised that while Susan and I were married. He was always very nice to me, so nice, in fact, that one had to conclude he was either very grateful to me for having taken Susan off his hands, or else that his feelings were so aggressive that he didn't dare let them out at all.'

'Why shouldn't it have been the first?' I asked.

'Ah, you'd think that, of course, you're so jealous of Susan. I can quite see you'd prefer it like that. But it wasn't the case. When Susan and I broke up, perhaps it was rather like that. Our marriage had been a bad mistake. She wasn't at all what I'd really been looking for, though she was so beautiful it took me a little while to find it out. I think beauty's awfully important. I went on being in love with her beauty for ages after she left me. I think I'm cured now, but for a long time it was terrible. In other ways, though, I was quite glad Piers turned up, because I don't think I could ever have faced hurting Susan by simply leaving her myself, and I think I might have gone mad if I hadn't.'

'Was it really as bad as that?' Curiously enough, I felt more annoyed than seemed reasonable. I should have gone quite mad myself, living with Susan, but that is the right of a sister.

'It was pretty bad,' said Sholto, 'pretty bad. She used to say and do things that I'll never forgive. For instance, she had a name for me—' He stopped.

'Yes?' I had heard most of this before, but the name was new to me.

'It was horrible,' he said.

'What was it?'

'It—it was Pussy.'

'Pussy?'

He nodded, his eyes avoiding mine in embarrassment. 'What's so really terrible about that?' I asked. 'It's not very dignified but it could easily have been worse.'

'It was short for something,' he said.

'For what?'

'I'll never tell you that—never as long as I live!' he said with extraordinary violence.

70

'Ah well, you're quite happy about it all now, aren't you?' I said. 'After all, you never really liked being married.'

He gave his little peculiar grin. 'You may be quite right. I'm selfish about money and I don't like washing-up. All the same, one ought to be married, I think.'

'Why?' I asked.

'Well, people always think there's something peculiar about a person who doesn't get married.'

'But suppose there is?'

'You think I'm peculiar?'

I do not think I have ever met a person whom I did not think peculiar, but that is a complicated matter to go into fully. I answered. 'I do think there's something peculiar about your coming here to find this picture. There's something too altruistic about it. It isn't entirely like you. What d'you get out of it, Sholto?'

He looked disappointed at the slight shift of subject, for there was never anything Sholto liked talking about so much as what one thought about him. 'What are *you* getting out of it?' he asked.

'That's different,' I said. 'I've let Susan bully me all my life. I'm too used to it to resist.'

'She bullies me too,' said Sholto.

'And that's all there is to it? She told you to come and you came?'

'That's all.'

71

'Queer that she didn't put Piers up to it too, don't you think?'

He wrinkled his narrow forehead at me and after a moment got up and walked towards the fire, turning his back on me and remaining silent so long that I wondered what unexpected thing my question had done to him. At last he turned round again.

'I don't like talking about Piers,' he said. 'Let's talk about me.'

I yielded to the inevitable. 'Go ahead.'

'D'you think there's anything against my getting married again?'

'Nothing whatever, if that's what you want to do.'

'But I'm not sure that I do.'

'I don't think I follow you.'

'Well, I can't help worrying about it, somehow.'

'Who's the woman?'

'I can't quite make up my mind. There are two ... And there's another I met last week. She's absolutely beautiful, but that's all I know about her. Beauty's awfully important though, isn't it? I'm awfully easily put off by a bad figure or an ugly skin. The one I thought I was in love with is really just a bit too fat.'

'I thought you said you never met any women.'

'Well, I never meet the one I really want.'

'What about this beautiful one you just mentioned?'

'I've an idea there's already another man on the scene.'

'You might compete.'

'But that's always too much trouble.'

'Then the situation's really very difficult.'

He gave a deep sigh. 'It's awful. But if only I could meet the perfect woman ....'

'I suppose there's no hope that you'll ever grow up?' I said.

'None whatever, I should think,' he answered. 'I'll be adolescent till I die.'

That was one of the things I always liked about Sholto. Though he was not quite certain that he liked being as preposterous as he was, he never pretended to be anything else. At a certain level, he had an uncommon honesty.

This often made him shrewder than one would have thought at seeing through other people's make-beliefs. Remembering this, I suddenly asked him, 'Sholto, what d'you really think about Norman's reason for keeping Susan out of the house? The picture doesn't explain it, even if he's got it.'

But this was changing the subject again from the only one that mattered, and with a look of irritation, he answered, 'Oh, I should think it's just the picture.'

'But it's got something to do with Beryl—'

The face Sholto suddenly made at me stopped me. He was grimacing at the door. I turned and saw Norman standing there.

I thought he looked as if he had not slept

73

well. His face had a dull, pasty look. But it was freshly shaved, and he was wearing a well-pressed grey suit. I do not believe I have ever seen Norman untidy. He had an expression of pleasant surprise at seeing Sholto.

'Nobody told me about this,' said Norman. 'When did you get here?'

'Well, as a matter of fact, in the middle of the night,' said Sholto. 'I hope I'm not in the way.'

'No, no, I'm delighted to see you,' said Norman. 'It's the season for visitors, I gather.'

'I'm afraid it looks as if I've eaten your breakfast,' said Sholto.

'Never mind, we'll see what Mrs Fawcett can do about it,' said Norman. 'Luckily she never fusses. A treasure of a woman.' He rang the bell. 'Are you staying long?'

'No, of course not,' said Sholto. 'I just dropped in—'

'Oh, you must stay,' said Norman. 'At any rate—' He smiled from Sholto to me. 'You must stay till I begin to understand the reason for these visitations. I begin to think there's more in them than meets the eye.'

Sholto began to get confused. 'If I'd known Marabelle would be here, I'd never have planted myself on you at the same time.'

'Why, don't you like Marabelle?' Norman asked.

'Yes—no—I mean that isn't what I meant. I meant you don't want the whole house littered up with people,' said Sholto.

74

'But I love it,' said Norman.

I stood up. 'I think I'll go and get dressed,' I said.

'Just a minute,' said Norman. 'You were talking about a picture as I came in—'

'*Scott of the Antarctic*,' said Sholto promptly.

'That's right,' I said. 'Both of us go to pictures far too much.' I made for the door.

It opened just before I reached it and Mrs Fawcett came in. As Norman started negotiations with her for some breakfast, I slipped past her and went out into the hall.

I never knew what hit me, but the next moment I was lying flat on the floor, and heard the noise of my own scream echoing through the house.

CHAPTER SEVEN

As I began to feel certain that I had not broken any bones, I realised that Norman, Sholto and Mrs Fawcett were standing over me and that Basil was squatting on the floor beside me, looking as if he were threatening to start applying artificial respiration.

'God, can't she yell!' said Sholto. 'I'd never have believed it.'

'Basil,' said Mrs Fawcett sternly, 'I told you not to.'

75

'Are you all right, Marabelle?' asked Norman.

I sat up and rubbed my knees, which had suffered the most.

'What happened?' I asked.

'It was my fault, Mrs Baynes,' said Basil. 'I'm terribly sorry. I do hope you aren't hurt. I'd never have done it if I'd thought for a moment—'

'The trouble with you, Basil,' Norman interrupted, 'is that you think too much. I keep telling you not to.'

'You see, I was tidying this cupboard here,' said Basil, 'and I was just pulling out this tool-box when you came out suddenly and tripped right over it.'

'Who told you to tidy the cupboard, Basil?' asked Norman.

'Nobody as a matter of fact, Mr Rice,' said Basil, 'but it does want doing. And I found something in it … Mrs Baynes, is this the picture you were looking for?'

I heard Sholto catch his breath. He moved forward quickly to look over my shoulder at the picture Basil started pulling out of the cupboard from behind a heap of junk of the kind that collects in cupboards, even in well-ordered households. The picture was in a heavily moulded gilt frame and was of some Highland cattle paddling at the edge of a loch.

Norman chuckled. '*Were* you looking for that picture, Marabelle? I'd love to give it

76

to you.'

'No,' I said. 'I wasn't looking for that.'

'What shall I do with it, then?' asked Basil. 'Shall I hang it somewhere? It'd look nice on the stairs, wouldn't it?'

'Just put it back in the cupboard and forget about it,' said Norman, 'and try to control this passion for tidying things that are quite comfortable as they are.'

'But one can't clean a place that's untidy,' said Basil fretfully.

'I don't see why not,' said Norman. 'Anyway, why clean inside a cupboard that never gets opened anyway?'

'Doesn't it get opened?' asked Basil. 'In that case I'll just take out a few things I've found in it and put them somewhere else. This box of tools, for instance. They're nice tools—they'll come in useful.'

Norman looked at him suspiciously. 'What are you plotting to use tools on in this house?'

A pale blush tinged Basil's cheeks. 'Oh, nothing in particular,' he said lightly, 'but you might like me to mend something sometime.' He picked up the box of tools and plunged into a small cloakroom beside the front door. 'I'll put it on this shelf here,' he said. 'It's nice and convenient.'

Norman turned back into the kitchen and Sholto and I followed him, while Mrs Fawcett returned to the kitchen to concoct Norman's breakfast.

'A nice boy, Basil,' said Norman, 'but very uncontrolled. I actually keep my study locked nowadays till he goes home, because nothing else will prevent him spreading a devastation of tidiness inside. And now—' He sat down at the head of the table and looked from Sholto to me. 'About this picture,' he said, 'and I don't mean *Scott of the Antarctic*.'

Sholto and I looked at one another. We both shook our heads.

'You'd rather not tell me?' said Norman.

'There's nothing to tell,' I said, while I racked my brain for a story.

'You'd told Basil something or other about some picture,' said Norman.

'He got it wrong,' I said. 'We had a chat while I was having breakfast, and I was telling him about that picture of Piers Beltane's—the one Susan made you buy and that you gave away to Dr Chappell when he got married. Basil must have misunderstood me and thought I wanted the picture myself or something.'

Norman gave me a long look, then nodded. 'I see.'

Fortunately it is very easy to lie to a courteous man, even when you know that he does not believe you.

I went out once more, crossed the hall safely this time and went upstairs to get dressed. I still had not decided what I was going to do, go home or stay, and I felt that it was time that I

78

made up my mind.

Sitting down by the electric fire, I thought that it would be best if I made up my mind before dressing, because I always find that my mind works most clearly straight after breakfast, before I have started doing anything else. When I wrote my play, that was the part of the day that I always used for it. Somehow, once I am dressed, I feel that the world can make calls on me of all kinds, and the risk of this happening tends to upset the never very powerful flow of my intellectual processes.

Lighting a cigarette, I tried to make my mind come to grips with the various problems before me. There seemed to me to be only one of importance. Did I care enough who had the Roger Clegg, Norman or Susan, to interfere any further? Examining my feelings carefully, I decided that I did not care at all, and that suggested that I should go home by a morning train. As soon as I had thought this, I made up my mind to stay.

It took me some minutes to discover why this should have happened, apart from the fact that that is often how I come to decisions. In fact, it was only while I was thinking rather vaguely of going over to have a gossip with Millie Weinkraut that the point clarified itself. I remembered then that I did not know for certain that Norman had the picture, and if he had not got it, it remained as mysterious as ever why he should suddenly have refused Susan admittance to his house.

At lunch I saw Norman and Sholto again, but the subject of pictures was avoided. After lunch Norman went to his study, Sholto went to sleep on the sofa in the room Basil called the lounge, and I went to see Millie. I wanted, besides other things, to use her telephone. Norman's telephone was in his study, so that to ring up Susan on it and speak freely would not have been possible.

Millie was in her kitchen when I arrived, doing some ironing. She heard me at the door and when I told her from the hall what I wanted, called out to me to go ahead. Settling myself by the telephone, expecting a conversation of some length, I put a call through to Susan's flat.

Piers answered it, and I thought there was a hesitation in his voice before he said he would go and see if Susan was in. But Susan, it seemed, came in a hurry, and started speaking breathlessly before I could even begin.

'I've been hoping you'd ring me,' she said. 'Tell me quickly, have you seen the picture?'

'No,' I said, 'but—'

'Have you been looking for it?'

'No, but Sholto has, and he hasn't seen it either. Now listen, Susan—'

Her voice broke in in a squeak from the other end. 'Did you say *Sholto*?'

'Yes, of course.'

'Oh God!' she said and there was a pause.

'Now listen, Susan,' I began again, 'I want to make it clear that I don't care a damn one way or the other about the picture, and I'm moderately resentful at having been sent down here by a sob-story about Norman refusing to let you see your children—'

'Wait,' she said imperatively. 'Wait, I want to think. Did you say Sholto's there, looking for the picture?'

'Of course he's here,' I said. 'You sent him, didn't you?'

'I certainly did not.'

'What?'

'I happened to meet him after I'd seen you, and I told him about the picture being missing, but I never said a word to suggest he should go and look for it. As if I would!'

'I don't believe you,' I said flatly.

She went on rapidly, 'Don't be a fool. Would I have asked him to look for it when I'd already asked you?'

'You hadn't already asked me. You'd asked me to find out why Norman wouldn't let you see your children. You only let me know about the picture this morning.'

'Yes, I know—but in my own mind I'd asked you already. Marabelle, you mustn't let Sholto find the picture. I don't know what he's up to, but it's something to annoy me.'

'Shall I tell you what I think, Susan?' I said. 'You were just a little bit afraid that when I got your letter and found out why you really sent

81

me down here, I'd come straight home. So you thought suddenly of sending Sholto.'

'You're talking absolute nonsense,' she answered. 'As if I could *send* Sholto. He'd never do anything for me, even when we were married. He's a completely selfish person. And I knew you wouldn't be annoyed—you're much too much of an angel.'

'I was very annoyed—and I'm not going to bother about the picture.'

'Oh, Marabelle, you must!'

'No.'

'But listen, Marabelle, the picture isn't important for it's own sake. I might even let Norman keep it if he wants it so badly. And don't you see, what I really and truly wanted you to go down there for was to get Norman to stop this absurd business of not letting me into the house. And as long as he has the picture hidden away somewhere he won't let me in for fear I might find it. So the picture's got to be found before we can straighten up anything else.'

'It doesn't make sense to me,' I said. 'I can't see Norman wanting anything so badly that he'd do a thing like that.'

'You don't know him like I do,' she said. 'All those very quiet, even-tempered people who seem to take everything as it comes without making a fuss have bees in their bonnets of one sort or another. Norman's bee is pictures. You know he hasn't got taste in anything else—he

82

couldn't live in that awful house if he had—but he thinks about pictures a lot. I don't know how often he's tried to get the Clegg out of me. Well, I suppose when he was alone in the sitting-room here the other day he suddenly couldn't resist the temptation and just took it without stopping to think out what it would mean. I'm sure he never thought then that he'd have to stop me seeing Maurice and Beryl. But he's awfully stubborn in his own way, and once he's taken up a position, it's awfully difficult to get him to shift from it.'

That at least I knew was true. But it all seemed to me too complicated to be convincing. I did not believe in Susan's anxiety that Sholto should not find the picture, I did not believe that Norman, who had put up with so much else, would let a picture come between Susan and her children. I was not even sure whether or not to believe that the picture was missing. I was inclined to think that I was being used in some peculiar scheme of Susan's, directed towards making Norman do something that he had refused to do, or which she thought he would refuse to do.

Yet there was an unusual amount of emotion in her voice as she went on, 'Is there any reason why you shouldn't just stay and look round for the picture, Marabelle? Don't say anything about it to Norman, then if it isn't there, no harm will have been done. On the other hand, if you find it, you can slip away with it quietly, without hurting his feelings. *Please*, Marabelle—it's so important to me.'

'Well,' I said hesitantly, 'perhaps I'll just look around, but—'

'Oh, I knew you would!'

'But even if I find it, I'm not going to touch it.'

'Oh, you are a dear! I can't tell you, I can't possibly tell you, how grateful I am. Piers wanted me to go to the police and report the loss, and perhaps that's what I'll do in the end if you can't find it, but you see, I can't possibly do that until I'm absolutely sure that Norman hasn't got it, and though I know it sounds absurd to think of him stealing it, still there's just enough circumstantial evidence to be worrying ... Thank you so much, Marabelle.'

Putting the telephone down, I thought what a very odd mind Susan had. The argument she had dropped casually into her last few sentences seemed to me by far the best she had given me.

I went into the kitchen to pay up for the call. Millie was just finishing the ironing and told me to wait while she made some tea.

'I couldn't help hearing most of that,' she said.

'Then I wonder if you made any better sense out of it than I did,' I said. 'I suppose you or Ernst haven't heard anything from Norman about a picture by Roger Clegg?'

'I've heard him speak of it,' she said.

84

'When?' I asked.

'Oh, often.'

'Has he said anything about it recently—during the last few days, I mean?'

'Not that I remember,' she said. 'But we don't see as much of Norman as we used to. Ernst thinks it's because he isn't well, but I'm not quite sure. We had a sort of row with him not long ago—at least Ernst did—and though it's supposed to have been patched up, I sometimes think that something Ernst said may be rankling in Norman's mind.'

'They seemed quite friendly yesterday evening.'

'Oh yes—as I said, it's supposed to have been patched up. And Ernst says there's nothing wrong, but then he mightn't notice. He says awfully sarcastic things sometimes without thinking of what other people may really feel. He never means any harm, but people do get offended sometimes.'

'What was the row about?'

'St Ambrose, of course. Ernst never quarrels about anything else.'

'Ah no, I should have known. But I didn't know Norman knew anything about St Ambrose.'

'Well, one never knows what he'll get on to next with that funny book he keeps writing. I don't suppose he'll ever finish it, do you?'

'There doesn't seem much reason why he should,' I agreed. 'He's been at it for about

85

twelve years.'

'Ernst has been writing about St Ambrose for fifteen years,' said Millie with a trace of pride.

'Then it's neck and neck. Millie—'

'Yes?' She disconnected the iron.

'I can't quite explain the feeling I've got, but I'm worried. I've felt it ever since I got down here yesterday. I think I'm going to tell you about it, if you don't mind.'

'All right,' she said. 'Just wait till I make this tea.'

'I can't see that there's actually anything to worry about,' I went on, 'yet I can't get rid of the feeling that there's something badly wrong here. Of course, a number of people are behaving in a rather preposterous way, but then they always have, so it can't be that.'

'I don't know,' she said. 'Sometimes one can take it and sometimes one can't.'

'But I don't think I'm unduly given to worrying about such things,' I said.

'Well, John's away, and you aren't used to that,' she said.

That had not occurred to me, but it seemed all of a sudden to make very good sense. I sat there thinking it over while Millie made the tea.

We took it into the sitting-room and sat down in front of the huge brick fireplace and I began to tell Millie everything that had happened since Susan's visit yesterday. I had always found Millie a comfortable person to talk to. Her eyes dwelt intently on one's face and she did not interrupt, while her thoughts slipped away into agreeable dreams of antique furniture, which kept the expression on her face very calm and pleasant and friendly. I do not think she ever bothered to listen to more than a quarter of what any one said to her, but now and then she would grunt as if she were taking it all in. She never made me feel that I was talking too much or boring her.

When at last I came to the end of my story, she said nothing for a while. I did not mind. Talking had done me good. I had vented a good deal of spite against Susan and was feeling much the better for it, and I was ready to change the subject. So on the whole I was gratified when all she said was, 'I believe I'd hate to have a housekeeper. When I was younger I used to think it'd be wonderful to have someone else to do all the work for one, but I shouldn't like it really.'

I discovered I had forgotten all about feeling worried for some time, and we sat talking disconnectedly.

It was beginning to grow dusk already when I went back to the other house. Several of its windows were lit up, among them the window of Norman's study. The curtains were not drawn, and on a sudden thought, I decided to walk past. It had just occurred to me that if I could snatch a quick look round the room, perhaps unnoticed by Norman, I should be able to see if the Clegg was hanging on one of the walls.

But I was unlucky. As I came abreast of the window, Norman appeared at it and jerked the thick curtains together. He saw me too.

He paused. Then he opened the window a little way.

'Come in,' he said gravely. 'I want to talk to you. I want you to tell me what you and Sholto are really doing here.'

CHAPTER EIGHT

I said, 'All right,' and stepped in at the window. I looked all round the room. The Clegg was not there. The room looked just as it always had, with the big desk and half the floor a mix-up of books, cuttings from newspapers, snippets of typescript, jars of paste, scissors and the appearance of having been sprayed with paper-clips.

'Now,' said Norman, 'what's it all about?'

'I'll speak only for myself,' I said, 'because I'm not absolutely sure what Sholto's up to.'

'I don't suppose any one ever is, least of all himself.' Norman pushed forward a chair and gave me a cigarette. 'However, you seem to have a joint interest in a picture, and I seem to come into it somewhere.'

I sat down. 'It's Susan's Clegg.' I had

decided to tell him the truth. 'It's missing and she thinks you've got it. She thinks that's why you won't let her into the house. You know she won't go to the police about it and that as long as you can prevent her finding it, you can keep it. She didn't tell me this yesterday when she asked me to come down here, she only said she wanted me to find out why you suddenly wouldn't let her see her children. I found out what she really wanted by letter this morning, and this afternoon I went over to the Weinkrauts and had a talk with her on the telephone. She said she might even let you keep the picture if you want it so badly, provided you stop this business of keeping her out of the house. She said she never asked Sholto to do anything in the matter at all, but I've no idea whether or not that's true. And I may as well tell you too that I haven't found the Clegg and haven't yet looked very hard for it.'

I suppose I had spoken excitedly. Norman's eyebrows seemed to go higher and higher while I spoke, then he made me say it all over again. By the time I finished the second time he was frowning.

'The only sense I can make of the thing,' he said, 'is that the Clegg appears to be missing, and that seems to me a serious matter. I think the police should be called in without delay.'

'That's what Piers thought,' I said.

'For once he was right.'

'But Susan won't do it as long as she believes

89

you've got it.'

'Very kind of her. But I don't happen to have it.'

'Unfortunately,' I said, 'it disappeared just after your visit to her flat.'

'Did it indeed!' He chewed a thumb nail. 'It sounds to me as if Piers must have pawned it and is trying to put the blame on me.'

'That doesn't really seem likely,' I said. 'Piers has plenty of money.'

'No one has plenty of money—it's a state of mind that doesn't exist. However, I agree, the idea's a bit unlikely—almost as unlikely as that I should go to Susan's flat and steal something that belonged to her.'

'But you've done something else which a week ago I should have considered most unlikely,' I said. 'You suddenly won't have your ex-wife in the house.'

'And two unlikelys make a likely?'

'They might.'

'Yes, perhaps they might,' he agreed. 'There's truth in that. But it happens that this time they don't.'

'Then why *are* you keeping Susan out of the house, Norman?'

I am not sure whether his appearance of not having heard me was natural or assumed.

'And you're sure the Clegg's really missing?' he said. 'This isn't some curious gambit of Susan's?'

'I think I'm sure,' I said. 'I think she's really

worried about it—and about the children.'

'Then I think the police should be called in without delay,' he said. 'If she doesn't do that, I shall.' His hand went out to the telephone.

I said quickly. 'You aren't going to do that straight away, are you, without consulting her?'

'No, it was Susan I was going to ring up,' he said. 'I was going to tell her that if she hasn't notified the police by tomorrow morning, I'll do it myself. But wait a minute . . .' He sat back. 'I want to think.'

'You know, I don't think even your ringing up the police will convince Susan that you haven't got the picture,' I said. 'She'll only think you've had time to cache it somewhere.'

He gave me an amused look. 'And is that what you think too?'

I smiled back at him without answering. This seemed a sensible thing to do, since I did not know what I thought.

'Well, well,' he said, 'it appears that I'm thought a very competent criminal. But I haven't got that picture, Marabelle.'

'Then why won't you have Susan here?'

I saw a quickly suppressed look of distress in his eyes. He turned his head away. His hand went out to the telephone and fingered it hesitantly. 'That picture's valuable,' he muttered. 'If it's lost or stolen, I want it found. I don't want it used as a pawn in some irresponsible game of Susan's.'

'But I'm not sure that that's how she's using it,' I said. 'I've got a feeling that the thing's missing and that she's honestly worried about it.'

He gave an abrupt laugh. 'But can't you see what she might be up to? Doesn't it stare you in the face?'

'No,' I said.

'Then you aren't as quick as I thought. If Susan wanted to upset me and get me to see her and discuss my decision with her, what more cunning method could she have chosen than this? She knows how much I care about that picture. Didn't I almost ring her up just now?'

'Then you don't think the picture's missing at all?'

He shifted irresolutely. 'That's the trouble, I'm not sure. And if it's genuinely lost, I want the police told immediately. I'll have to think.'

'But Norman, about not seeing Susan—'

He interrupted me with a quick gesture and an unusual look of anger. 'That's my business.'

'Yes.'

The look vanished. 'I'm sorry you've been dragged into this,' he said. 'It wasn't fair on you. And I'll just tell you one thing...' But he hesitated before he went on to tell it, eyeing me curiously. 'Marabelle, when Susan left me, why d'you think I let her go on coming here whenever she liked and turned myself into a sort of older brother instead of a husband? You've always kept your opinion to yourself on the subject, but tell me now, why did you think I did that?'

'I'm not sure that I ever tried to think it out,' I said.

'But you thought it queer, didn't you?'

'I'm not sure that I did. I'm not sure that one hasn't got to think that every one's queer all the time or else that nobody is. And I'm not sure which of those two attitudes is my normal way of thinking.'

'Well, I had a very simple reason for what I did,' he said. 'This is what I thought. I thought, I married a woman twenty years younger than myself, and there was always a risk that sooner or later she'd fall in love with someone of her own age—I've no right to complain too much now that it's happened. And there are the children. They oughtn't to lose their mother entirely. And I didn't like the idea of an arrangement whereby they should go and stay with her an agreed number of months in the year. I saw that turning into a competition between Susan and me for their affection, and perhaps Beryl and Maurice getting separated from one another in the process, and perhaps—perhaps I saw myself losing the competition, Marabelle ... And so I thought the best thing all round would be for Susan to come here freely whenever she wanted to, and for the children to go to her and come back here as they liked. The point is, this arrangement was entirely for the children—

and for myself in relation to them. And it was always on the cards that sooner or later I should come to the conclusion that the arrangement wasn't working.'

'Yes,' I said. 'But all the same ... Well, it's taken you a long time to come to this conclusion.'

He patted my hand. 'That's all I'm going to tell you.'

I stopped arguing. It seemed to me that after what he had said I could hardly go on.

He had given me a hint, however. He had made it clear that Susan had done something, or was doing something which he considered detrimental to the children, or to his relationship with them. I thought of Beryl's visit to Susan, and of Beryl's new hair-do and clothes. Could it be that he thought these were the first steps in making Beryl's morals the same as her mother's? Yet, come to think of it, Susan's moral tone was pretty high. Like Henry the Eighth, she always wanted marriage. I believe she must have been almost as idealistic about men as Henry must have been about women, believing that perfect happiness existed and could be made to sign on the dotted line if only one went on looking long enough.

The oddest part of it all was still Norman's refusal to explain his change of attitude to Susan. To do her justice, it was never difficult to explain awkward things to Susan, since she never took in more than she liked, thus making it next to impossible to hurt her. Whatever Norman had told her, I thought, she would have ended by finding it creditable to herself, and liking him all the better for it. Hers was a very comfortable sort of mind to have. Or had I got something wrong there, I wondered suddenly. Anyway, I had done what I could for her, and I should go home in the morning and start in earnest on my painting and distempering.

Nothing much more happened that evening. Beryl came home just before dinner, looking rosy and tired and surprisingly cheerful. She dashed off to her room to peel off her gardening clothes, and then to the bathroom, and I heard her singing in it. When she came down, she had on the same green dress that she had worn the evening before, and with the high colour in her cheeks and an air of contented tiredness about her, she looked bewilderingly lovely.

She kissed Norman casually and curled up in a corner of the sofa with a glass of sherry. She seemed to have forgotten that she had wanted to consult me about something. At dinner she got into a good-humoured argument with Sholto about education. Beryl, it appeared to-night, thought education a mistake. The right thing, she thought, was to dig the earth and plant things and make them grow, like a man called Tom, who was foreman on the market garden where she was working. Sholto reacted so apprehensively that it was plain he felt he himself was being threatened with having to adopt this terrible occupation. That was one of Sholto's troubles in life. He always thought that any opinion was pointed personally at him. After dinner, Ernst appeared again and he and Sholto and Norman played cut-throat, while I found a detective story to read and Beryl did some mending.

Again that evening, after the card-playing had stopped and Ernst gone home and Beryl had gone up to bed, Mrs Fawcett brought Norman his hot milk. He drank it quickly, and as if he were avoiding further talk with Sholto and me, said good night and went off to his room.

I went on reading my detective story. Sholto sat in silence for some minutes, idly shuffling the pack of cards and looking as if at any moment he might make them disappear into the air or change into a stream of coloured handkerchiefs, then he leant forward, picked up Norman's cup and smelt it.

'Milk,' he said, with disgust.

'Just milk,' I said.

'Sure?' he asked.

'What d'you mean?'

'Nothing in particular,' he said. 'Marabelle—'

'Well?'

'You haven't found the picture, I suppose?'

96

'No. I don't think Norman's got it. He says he hasn't.'

'Good Lord, you don't mean you asked him about it?'

'I did.'

'What a fool you are,' he said petulantly.

'No—I just don't believe he's got it,' I said. 'And Sholto, I spoke to Susan on the telephone, and she says she never asked you to come here and look for the picture.'

'She would,' he said. 'I don't believe that woman's ever known the meaning of the word gratitude in her life.'

'Then she did ask you, did she?'

He picked up the cup again and gazed at the few drops left at the bottom. 'D'you know, I can't think why a person should drink milk if they can drink something else,' he said.

'Health reasons,' I said. 'Sholto—'

'My health would have to be pretty bad before I'd drink it. Can't bear the stuff. Never could, even as a child.'

'So Susan didn't ask you to come down here?'

'Of course she did.'

I tucked my book under my arm and stood up. 'Funny how one often can't make oneself tell a direct lie till one's thought the matter over for a minute or two. Good night, Sholto.'

He gave the sudden, sharp-cornered grin that made his face engaging, 'Good night.'

'I wonder what you're up to,' I said. 'I

97

wonder what Susan's up to. I wonder what Norman's up to. And how I wish I'd never come.'

I slept better than night, perhaps because I went on reading my detective story for about an hour before I tried to sleep. In spite of the fact that a few minutes after I had turned off the light and settled down I heard footsteps overhead in a room which I knew was only a disused attic, I fell quickly into a comfortable sleep. The footsteps, I thought drowsily, must be those of Sholto, again looking for the bathroom in the wrong direction. But this time I did not bother to get up and put him right.

The next morning I again thought it would be a good idea to get up early and make my own coffee before Mrs Fawcett could appear and take a hand in it. But I was later than I had been the morning before, and as I went into the kitchen, Basil was just letting himself in at the back door, clutching several bottles of milk in his arms and holding a beautiful yellow rose between his lips, like a Spanish dancer.

He put the bottles down on the kitchen table and gave me the rose.

'I found it on the window-sill,' he said. 'I'm sure it's for you.'

I thought too that it probably was, but I asked, 'What makes you think that?'

'Because I never found roses on the window-sill till you came,' he said.

I felt rather glad to hear that Ernst did not

leave roses for Mrs Fawcett, and this feeling made me generous. I asked Mrs Fawcett, when she came in presently, if she would like the rose to put on the mantelpiece amongst her photographs.

But she shook her head. 'Thank you, but I don't hold with flowers in a kitchen,' she said. 'The steam kills them. They wither and die before their time. I can't bear to see flowers dying bit by bit. Really I'd sooner not have them in the house at all, it makes me so sad to see the petals fall. I don't like flowers on graves either really. What I like is a nice plain marble headstone, and then just the green grass. There's nothing makes me so sad as an untidy-looking grave with a lot of dying flowers.'

'I'm sorry,' I said, hurriedly putting the rose on my tray, 'I didn't mean to put such melancholy thoughts in your head.'

'That's quite all right, quite all right, Mrs Baynes,' she said with dignity. 'After all, us old people, we all have sad thoughts. We've seen so many people just wither away.' She picked up the bottles of milk that Basil had left on the table and put them into the refrigerator. 'It's the ones that go slowly that make me saddest,' she said. 'I remember Mr Pertwee, the gentleman I was with before I went to Mr Godstowe—'

'What did he die of?' I asked.

'Stomach,' she said. 'Or so the doctor said. I thought myself—'

99

'And did he die slowly?'

'Yes, nearly a year he took to die.'

'Did he leave you any money?'

'Now it's funny you should ask that,' she said, 'because he did leave me a small sum, just to show his appreciation of the way I looked after him during his last illness. He said to me, "I never knew what a treasure I'd got in the house," he said, "till I got ill, Mrs Fawcett—"'

I interrupted, 'I'm going to ask you a very personal question.' I did not know why my heart had started pounding. Perhaps it was this talk fit for a charnelhouse before I had my breakfast, and all begun by an innocent offer of a rose. 'Did Mr Fawcett die of his stomach?'

She closed the door of the refrigerator with a sudden bang. 'Why no,' she said, 'no ...' She turned and walked out of the kitchen.

I added a pot of marmalade to my tray. I picked it up and started up to my bedroom. A very curious thought had just come into my head and I wanted to get away by myself to think about it.

I heard Basil whistling happily in the sitting-room as he laid the fire. Mrs Fawcett was in the dining-room; I caught the flicker of white linen as she spread the cloth on the table. I went upstairs, and I was just outside my bedroom door when I heard footsteps on the staircase that led up to the attics. I paused, wondering if it was credible that Sholto had spent the whole night up there, hunting for the picture.

Then I saw that I had been mistaken in thinking that it had been Sholto whose footsteps I had heard overhead in the night, for coming down the stairs towards me were Susan and Piers Beltane.

CHAPTER NINE

Piers was the daintiest thing in artists that I have ever seen. I always thought of him as about half Susan's size, though in fact he was only two or three inches shorter than she was. But he was built so finely, so delicately, his hands and his feet were so small, his body so slender, that I thought of him as something miniature, a pocket-size imitation of a human being.

He was always dressed with what at first sight appeared a rather charming casualness. In fact, endless care had gone into the choice of his clothes. He had a passion for beautiful textures. The tweed or flannel, the cotton or silk that he wore, was always noticeable for its exquisite quality.

This fineness of texture seemed to me to extend to Piers himself. The nut-brown skin of his face looked as if it were a better leather than other people's. His light brown hair seemed spun from superior silk. His deep blue eyes might have been made of some rare and peculiarly expensive kind of glass.

He and Susan both stood still when they saw me. Then, looking a trifle unsure of themselves, they came on down the passage.

'Good,' said Susan. 'I hoped we'd find you before we ran into any one else. We're both terribly hungry, we want some breakfast.'

'Fortunately,' I said, 'that has nothing to do with me. You'll find Mrs Fawcett in the kitchen.'

'Don't be silly,' said Susan. 'That woman won't do anything for me. She'll probably try to push me out of the house.'

'I should have thought you and Piers between you were quite strong enough to resist,' I said.

'Don't be silly—' Susan was beginning again when I went into my room and shut the door.

Susan came in after me.

'Please, Marabelle, be an angel and go down and make sure we can have something to eat,' she said. 'I'm absolutely starving and I haven't slept a wink. The camp-beds up in that attic are things of nightmare.'

'Well, didn't you buy them yourself?' I asked.

'Yes, but that was to put in a shelter, when we were expecting the war—and for other people to sleep on.'

'I don't think you ought to be here at all,' I said. 'Norman doesn't want you.'

'But I had to come when you told me Sholto

was here,' she said, frowning.

'Even though you asked him to come?'

'I didn't ask him.'

'I don't know which of you is lying,' I said.

'You see, I don't know what he's up to, but he must be up to something.' Susan sat down on the edge of the bed, reached for my pot of coffee, took the lid off and smelt it. 'Probably he's after the Clegg for himself. Not that he wants it, but he'll use it to blackmail me into doing something for him, or giving him twice its value ... Hand me that tooth-glass, Marabelle. This coffee smells wonderful. It's just what I need.'

I handed her the glass, she filled it and helped herself to one of my pieces of toast.

'Why not ask Piers in too?' I said bitterly.

'Good idea.' She raised her voice and called, 'Piers!' So we had a breakfast party round my bed, on a supply of toast and coffee intended only for me. I felt very bad about it.

'Norman hasn't got the picture,' I said viciously.

'How d'you know?' Susan asked.

'He says so.'

'Then you told him all about it!'

'I did, and I believe him when he says he hasn't got it. He's very worried about its loss and says you must call in the police at once.'

'A blind,' she said. 'He knows I'd never do anything to get him into trouble.'

Piers, who had a soft, pleasant voice and

who could look contented and unruffled even after a night on a camp bed in an attic, said mildly, 'He's absolutely right, of course. I told you straight away you ought to call in the police. You'll have to sooner or later, and then how you're going to explain this delay I haven't the faintest idea.'

Susan shook her head. 'Naturally you don't mind if Norman gets into trouble,' she said. 'In fact, you'll enjoy it, but I shan't.'

'I don't know why you should think I'll enjoy it,' he said. 'I've a great regard for Norman.'

Susan laughed sarcastically.

'But I have,' Piers went on. 'And I can scarcely be said to have anything against him. Now if it were the other way round—'

'Don't be a fool, you know you're horribly jealous of my past,' said Susan. 'Still, the important thing now is to decide what to do. Norman's been thoroughly put on his guard and he'll have hidden the picture somewhere, probably not in the house at all. Did he go out at all yesterday, Marabelle?'

'I don't know,' I said. 'I was out myself most of the afternoon at the Weinkrauts.'

She flung her hands up as if this had been a miracle of silliness on my part. 'Where can he have put it?' she said.

'His bank, probably,' said Piers with a smile.

'No, he'd never hide a stolen picture in a bank,' she said.

104

'Why not, if you won't call in the police?'

Her eyes narrowed uneasily. 'No, he wouldn't...' But she looked less sure of herself. 'What a rotten trick, if he has...' She drank some coffee, then noticed my cigarettes beside the bed and helped herself. 'I know what we'll have to do,' she said after a moment.

'That was always quite plain,' said Piers.

She frowned. 'What d'you mean?'

'Well, if you really won't call in the police, like a reasonable person,' he said, 'you'll have to blackmail him.'

She nodded. 'That's what I was thinking.'

'If you try to do anything of the sort,' I said, 'I shall tell him all about it.'

'But blackmail can be quite a friendly sort of thing, if you do it in the right way,' said Susan. She blew out a spiral of smoke. 'Now what hold have I got over him?'

'The children,' said Piers.

'Sometimes I think you've a pretty evil mind,' she said disgustedly. 'I don't want to do anything mean.'

He chuckled.

She repeated fiercely, 'I don't, I wouldn't hurt him for the world. I appreciate Norman—'

There was a tap on the door. It opened almost before I could reply, and Norman stood there.

The rage of a quiet and gentle person is a terrifying thing. I had never before seen

Norman in a rage. I had never seen him with a face strained and grey and eyes like sooty glass with a furnace behind them. His body had a trembling tautness and he had a look of intense pain as if his own anger were a crucifixion.

'Get out!' he said almost inaudibly. 'Get out!'

Susan sprang up and went towards him as if she were going to embrace him, then stood still half-way across the room.

'How—how did you know we were here?' she asked.

'I heard your voice,' he said, still in a very low tone, as if his throat had tightened too much to let the words out.

'Well, I'm sorry if it annoys you,' she said, 'but I've got to talk to you.'

'I'm not going to talk to you,' he said. 'Get out.'

'But, Norman—'

'And I mean all three of you.'

'But you must listen to me!' said Susan, beginning to recover herself. 'You can't simply come to my house and steal my picture, and suddenly forbid me to see my children, and believe that I shan't demand an explanation.'

'I didn't come to your house and steal your picture,' said Norman. 'I haven't got your picture, and if you don't do it yourself, I'm going to report its loss to the police this morning. But I don't in fact believe that the picture is missing at all. You're pretending that it's lost for some purpose of your own. And I've had enough of that kind of thing. You are to get out at once, all three of you.'

To me those furious, half-whispered sentences were extraordinarily frightening. Perhaps they were all the worse because I was mostly in sympathy with Norman and had begun to feel very guilty about being in his house.

But I doubt if Susan had ever felt guilty about anything in her life, and the anger of another person excited her.

'I'm not going to let you talk to me like that,' she said. 'You'll feel horribly sorry about it afterwards, and I shouldn't like that. No, we're going to talk it all over reasonably. You're going to tell me what you've done with the picture—Piers says you've put it in the bank, but I don't really believe that—' She stopped, because Norman had turned and walked out of the room.

I stood up. 'Well, that's that,' I said. 'Thank goodness. Now if you two will get out of my room, I'll get dressed, pack and remove myself as rapidly as possible.'

Susan might not have heard. She came slowly back across the room, sat down facing Piers and looked thoughtfully into his eyes.

'What do we do now?' she asked in a low voice.

'Give him time,' said Piers, and ran a hand caressingly down his own coat-sleeve, letting himself enjoy the rough texture of the tweed.

'But he told us to get out.'

'I think he's hardly likely to call in the police to enforce the order.'

'I'm not sure.' She spoke with unusual sobriety. 'I don't think I've ever seen him look like that before.'

'Just give him time.' Piers smiled and stroked his coat-sleeve.

Suddenly I could not stand it any more. I had always known that I did not like Piers, but I had never felt such a feeling of repulsion as at that moment. In a way I had rather admired him, because, of her three husbands, he seemed the best able to manage Susan. But now I saw that he had achieved this simply by being several degrees more unscrupulous than she was.

Picking up what was left of my packet of cigarettes, I put it in the pocket of my dressing-gown and went out. I intended to go looking for Norman, to apologise to him and to tell him that I was leaving as soon as I was able to get dressed. But as I went down the stairs I saw the front-door closing, and recognised by the shadow that I could see through the stained-glass panels that it was Norman who had just gone out. I thought that probably he was going to walk off the worst of his rage. At the same time I noticed that it had begun to rain. I saw Norman turn up the collar of his raincoat as he strode down the drive.

I went on downstairs. Reaching the bottom, something caught against my ankle, and I should have fallen, possibly breaking my neck, or at least an arm or a leg, if arms had not been extended just in time to catch me. The arms were Basil's. So was the blame for my fall.

'Oh dear, oh dear, what a frightful fool I am!' he said, nearly sobbing in distress as he made sure that I was standing safe and undamaged on my own feet. 'I was just doing out the cloakroom, and I stood the mop here for a moment while I was moving these coats, and it must have fallen ....'

In fact the mop had fallen so that it made a perfect booby-trap at the bottom of the stairs.

'Please, Mrs Baynes, I'm terribly sorry,' he went on, even more shaken than I was. 'You see, I start thinking of something while I'm working, and then I don't notice things. D'you know what I was thinking of just now?'

'To be absolutely fair and open with you, Basil, I haven't the faintest idea,' I answered.

'I was thinking that if this was my house, I should turn this cloakroom into a grotto.'

'A grotto?' I said.

'Yes, you see, it has a tiled floor and it's rather dark, which somehow seems right for a grotto, and there's running water laid on in the basin, which perhaps one could turn into a kind of fountain, and then one could have ferns in pots, hanging from the ceiling, and some mossy stones and so on.'

'And then what would one do with it?'

'Oh, one wouldn't do anything with it, one would just have it. Don't you think it's a good idea?'

'I'm not sure,' I said, 'but certainly you have nicer thoughts in your mind than any one else in this house.' I went into the kitchen and set about making myself another pot of coffee.

Mrs Fawcett was there, having her own breakfast. It consisted of thick, dark tea and some finnan haddock. She offered to make the coffee for me, but I hurriedly urged her not to disturb herself. I wondered if she knew yet of Susan's presence in the house. If she did, she did not refer to it. She seemed, indeed, less anxious than usual for conversation. Perhaps she was afraid that I might ask her another question about her husband.

The coffee was not yet made when Sholto walked into the kitchen. His appearance gave me a shock. He seemed to me to be in almost as desperate a condition as Norman had been when he walked into my bedroom. But Sholto was not pale and inarticulate. His face was flushed and he was talking loudly to himself as he came in. He showed no signs of objecting to Mrs Fawcett and me overhearing what he was saying, and gradually included us as hearers.

'... I could kill him, I could smash his brains in, I could take him by the neck and choke the life out of him.' As he spoke, he gave me an intent stare which went right through me to

110

some horrible fantasy beyond me. 'I could tear his tongue out with red-hot pincers, I could stick knives into him ....'

At that point it began to grow obscene, until Mrs Fawcett, going very white, exclaimed, 'Well, I never!'

'But I could,' said Sholto truculently. 'You don't know what I could do. And I'd chase him through hell to show him I didn't mind the consequences. Yes, I would. That's what I'd do, I'd chase him through hell ... Is that coffee?'

I nodded in silence.

'Good,' said Sholto, 'that's what I need. I'm feeling drunk.'

'You sound it,' I said.

He helped himself. I wondered how much of this second pot I should manage to keep for myself.

'But I'm not drunk,' he said. 'I haven't had anything. But I know what it means now—"Now could I drink hot blood..." I know what that means. D'you understand? I know what it feels like when one's going to commit a murder.'

'Goodness gracious,' said Mrs Fawcett.

'If you knew what I know,' said Sholto, gulping coffee, then grimacing because he had not put in enough sugar and pouring in another couple of spoonfuls. I dare say he would have liked even his hot blood sweetened. 'Yes, if you knew half of what I know ... But you don't. You only see a face, a body. You see movements, you hear a voice. But you don't think about the rotten spirit behind them. You're taken in by the surfaces of things. You hang on to your peace of mind, no matter what foulness is poisoning the air around you. Oh, I know you—I know what you're like.'

'You *are* drunk,' I said.

'I'm not,' he said. 'You're saying that only because you're afraid I'm going to see through you and give you away. Don't worry, don't worry, you've no need to be afraid of me. You've never done me any harm. But that man has, and so I'm going to murder him. I'll have to, to keep sane. I'll have to smash his brains in, or take him by the neck and choke the life out of him or—'

'For heaven's sake,' I said, 'what on earth has Norman ever done to you?'

'Norman?' said Sholto. 'It's Piers I'm going to murder.'

CHAPTER TEN

Mrs Fawcett said, 'Now, now, you shouldn't say things like that, it isn't right. What you want is a couple of aspirins and a lie-down. Not that we don't all feel like that some time or other. It's the food. We're undernourished and that upsets the nerves.'

Her tone, if not what she said, had some effect on Sholto, for he sat down abruptly and gave her a puzzled stare, as if he could not imagine what he had said to make her address him in this fashion.

She went on, 'It's all starch, that's the trouble. You put on weight but it doesn't do you any good.'

I said, 'When did you find out they were here, Sholto?'

'I heard their voices in your room,' he said. 'The door was open.' He said it a little more calmly, and Mrs Fawcett looked pleased with herself, as if it were she who had produced this result. Perhaps she had.

'If they give you one thing, they take away something else,' she said. 'They give you jam and they take away your sugar.'

'I didn't know you had such strong feelings about Piers,' I said.

'Didn't he take away my wife?' said Sholto.

'Yes, but I had the feeling that really you were rather relieved,' I said.

'Did you?' He said it in an odd tone. 'Perhaps I was. But we've all got pride, haven't we?'

'It's a troublesome thing to have when it contradicts our real feelings,' I said.

'All our feelings are real, even the contradictory ones,' he answered. 'In fact, those are the most real, because they're always out of control.'

113

'Well, I hope you're feeling better now,' I said.

'Not while that man's in the house.'

'Then why don't you leave?'

'As if I were leaving him a clear field again?' He laughed angrily. 'Besides, I'm feeling too sick to leave.'

'There,' said Mrs Fawcett. 'It's stomach, like I said.'

'It's my nerves,' said Sholto. 'Whenever I feel aggressive, I start feeling sick.'

'Aggressive somehow seems a mild word for the way you seemed to be feeling a moment ago,' I said.

'The way I'm still feeling.'

'Murderous strikes me as a better word.'

'If you like. And if I have to see him again, I probably shall murder him. Just the sight of him does something to me that I can't explain. To see him so self-satisfied and sure of himself, thinking he can have anything he wants ....'

'I know what you mean,' I said. 'But murder usually hits back at oneself, so I've been told.'

'That's if one's careless,' said Sholto. He reached out for the jug of coffee. Rather disturbed, I saw that his hand was trembling. Also I saw that his eyes still stared in a blind, intent way at some picture in his mind. So even if he were dramatising his hatred considerably to hold the attention of Mrs Fawcett and me, there was something real in it.

I realised that I had never considered before

114

what Sholto felt about Piers. Just then I was pleased by the discovery of this hatred. It eased some feeling in myself. But at that point I left him to the comfort of Mrs Fawcett, and went upstairs to my room. Susan and Piers had left it. I dressed and started packing my bag. I did not know the morning trains to London, but I was going to leave the house immediately. I could go to the Weinkrauts' and telephone from their house for a taxi.

I almost managed it. I had just straightened my hat at the mirror, and as an afterthought had pinned Ernst's yellow rose into my buttonhole, when Susan walked in.

She took a look at me and said, 'Good God, next time you want to buy a hat, you'd better let me know and I'll come along and help you.'

I could think of nothing more horrible. 'I like it,' I said, 'and so does John.'

'John's an angel,' she said. Then she saw my bag. She did not argue. She simply went over to it, opened it and started throwing its contents out on the bed.

I lost my temper and began to shout at her incoherently.

'You look hideous when you do that,' she remarked. 'Of course you aren't leaving yet. You and I are going to have a talk with Norman. You can always handle Norman, and it wouldn't be economical to have come here and gone away again without doing what you came for.'

115

'To hell with economy.'

'I hope that isn't a sentiment that grips you often,' she said, and of all things, began to give me a lecture on the dangers of wasting money. Meanwhile she had pushed my bag under the bed and was neatly fending off all my efforts to get at it.

'Anyway, what's the matter with my hat?' I asked, because she always succeeds in sowing doubts in my mind.

'It looks like a soup-plate decorated with some leftover Irish stew,' she said. 'Now let's go down and talk sensibly to Norman. I've sent Piers out for a walk, because he riles Norman. I think just you and me together will be able to make him see sense.'

'Norman's gone out for a walk too,' I said.

'That's a nuisance. Well, we'll have to wait, and Piers will have to go on keeping out of the way—' She broke off, listening. 'That was the front door,' she said. 'It'll be Norman coming back.' She gripped my arm with shockingly muscular fingers and pulled me towards the door. 'Come along.'

As usual I gave in, and we went downstairs. But it was not Norman who had just come in. It was Sholto who had just gone out. Susan said, 'Damn!' and stood still. Just then we heard a sound in the study and Susan started towards it. Norman was there, standing by the desk, vaguely turning over sheets of paper. Susan pulled me into the room after her and shut

116

the door.

'We're going to talk,' she said. 'You aren't going to get out of things like this. I'm going to find out what you've done with my picture.'

Norman was looking very old and very ill. With Susan looking buoyant and determined and, as usual, very beautiful, and improperly young, it was difficult to realise that they had ever been married. I felt so ashamed of myself for being there at all that I slithered quickly into a chair by the door and started looking hard at Norman's bookcases.

But I was surprised by Norman's voice when he spoke and quickly turned to look at him. The anger had gone from his tone; it was entirely calm and he spoke without hesitation or uncertainty.

'It would be far better for you, Susan,' he said, looking up into her eyes, 'not to press me to give you any explanations. It would be far better for you to go away and leave matters as they are. I am very sorry your picture has disappeared. It is possible that I'm even sorrier than you are. I'll do anything in my power to help you recover it. But I do not want you or your husband here in this house, and I do not want to be forced into giving you any explanation of this wish of mine. This is not perverseness on my part, but comes from serious consideration of your happiness. Please go. Please stop talking and go.'

It would have been too much to expect that

Susan would take any notice of what he said. In fact, I began to wonder what Norman meant, because he must have known that he could not have chosen a worse way to handle Susan.

Standing over him, she said, 'Listen, you can have the picture if you want it so much. If I'd known you were so crazy to have it that you'd do a thing like this, I'd have let you have it anyhow. Where is it? Let's go and get it and hang it up here where you can look at it all day long, if you want to—and then let's drop this nonsense about my not seeing Maurice and Beryl.'

'Susan, I haven't got your picture,' said Norman. There was an odd glitter in his eyes.

'I don't believe you,' she said.

'I'm sorry, because I'm telling you the truth,' he answered.

'If you were—' she began.

'Well?' he said, sounding as if he hoped she was going to see sense.

'If you were—which I don't believe—why should you suddenly have taken this new line about the children?'

'Let's not talk about that,' he said.

'But certainly, let's talk about just that!' she said excitedly. 'If you'd done this when I first left you, I'd have seen nothing strange in it. But you didn't. And now suddenly, without explanations, you change. It isn't fair to me.'

'Have you always been fair to me?'

'That isn't the point.'

118

'Why not?'

She looked surprised. 'Of course it isn't. A person like you doesn't behave in this way because all of a sudden he wants revenge because one hasn't been fair to him.'

'Thank you for your good opinion,' he said, rather tight-lipped. 'But I asked you just now not to press me for explanations, telling you that that was on the whole for your own good. I repeat that.'

'Oh, Norman, for heaven's sake—!' It was obvious that she would not take him seriously.

He had become even paler and was looking still more distraught, and I thought that his grip on himself might slip at any moment. The thought scared me. I had never seen it happen. 'I repeat—' he began.

She would not let him go on. 'I haven't done anything to make you stop me seeing the children. Have I? Have I done anything that gives you that right? Has any one told you I've done anything?'

'No,' he said, 'you haven't done anything.'

'Are you sure you believe that?' she said. 'Has any one been telling you anything— anything that isn't true?'

'No,' he said again.

'If any one has told you anything against me—'

'Stop, stop!' he shouted at her, jumping up and walking quickly away from her. He even began a gesture as if to cover his ears, but he

119

controlled it. 'Stop thinking about yourself for a moment. No one's talked to me about you. People have a way of not mentioning you to me if they can help it. I'm simply acting as I think best and I don't want to explain it to any one.'

'But Norman—'

It was the look on his face as he turned and started walking towards her once more that made her stop.

'All right then,' he said in a low voice, 'you can have it. It's been a temptation. I've thought to myself again and again that I'd like to see the look on your face when I told you. But I shan't like it really—or shall I?' He paused, looking intently into her face.

Susan took a step backwards. All of a sudden she had become as scared as I was.

'I don't know what's the matter with you,' she said. 'You aren't well—I believe that's the trouble. You aren't well and you're seeing something all out of proportion.'

'No, I'm not well,' he answered. 'I've not been well for a long time.'

'But Norman, you should have said—'

'It's made no difference,' he said, speaking more loudly, 'and my health has no more to do with this situation than the disappearance of your picture—if it really has disappeared. The truth is this, Susan. When Beryl went to visit you and stayed with you, your husband, Piers Beltane, made love to her whenever your back was turned. She came back here half in love

120

with him and half mad with distress at what had happened. That's why I told you I wouldn't have you here. I didn't in fact mind your seeing her, but I wanted to make sure she saw no more of Piers. And my reason for making the ban seem to be directed against you was to avoid the necessity of telling you precisely what I've told you this minute.'

Again Susan was looking at him as if she had not taken in anything he had said. But this time the appearance was false. She had heard it all. A blankness came into her eyes and her face grew empty of everything except a painful bewilderment. Norman turned away at once, as if he could not bear to look at it.

One of her hands made a meaningless gesture in the air before her. 'It isn't true,' she said. 'You're lying.'

Without looking round he shook his head.

'You must be lying,' she said more firmly. 'You're lying about the picture—and now—'

'For God's sake,' he cried explosively, 'will you forget about the picture for a moment. I didn't take it—'

There was a light tap at the door.

We all turned, startled, as if the sound had some extraordinary meaning. There was an instant of complete silence in the room. The door opened. It was Basil.

'Excuse me,' he said, 'I'm sorry to interrupt, but is this the picture you were looking for, Mrs Baynes?'

He held up before me a picture of four ladies having a picnic in a meadow.

'Yes,' I said, 'that's it.'

Norman and Susan were both staring at it and seemed unable to say a word.

'Where did you find it?' I asked.

Basil walked across to the desk and carefully laid the picture down upon it.

'I found it in the cloakroom,' he said, 'just this minute. I—I also found a gentleman in there. He's dead.' As he said it, his knees crumpled and he slid quietly to the floor.

CHAPTER ELEVEN

Norman went first. Then Susan and I gathered up our courage and went after him.

The dead man was Piers Beltane. He was lying on the floor with his face to the wall, on which hung a row of coats and mackintoshes. The back of his head was a horrible sight. There was a big hammer on the floor near him, lying in a puddle of blood. There was blood on the wall and the floor and on several of the coats hanging above him.

I saw all this with a dull clarity that later surprised me, but with a feeling that the real horror of the situation stirred in some hell just behind the appearance of things and might erupt in myself at any moment, making me do

122

some violent and inexplicable thing.

Norman pulled the door shut. Turning his back upon it, he went to Susan and took hold of her by the forearms, once more peering intently into her face. I think he expected her to collapse.

But Susan looked as if she had not yet recovered from the shock that she had had a moment ago in Norman's study. Her face still had the empty and bewildered look that it had had when Norman had told her his real reason for keeping her out of the house.

'But the picture,' she muttered stupidly, 'you had it all the time.'

He gave me a glance, then led her into the drawing-room. She went docilely and sat down and allowed herself to be given some whisky. So did I, and so did Basil, who had just appeared, rubbing his head where he had bumped it on the floor and muttering apologies for having fainted. I heard Norman say something about the police and I watched him go out. I heard the tinkle of the telephone in his study as he dialled.

'The queer thing is,' said Susan a moment after he had gone, looking at me with a blurred, puzzled stare, 'that I knew it all the time—about Piers and Beryl.'

I said nothing.

She went on, 'I knew what Piers was doing before Beryl left. But I didn't want to admit it to myself. That's why I made such a fuss about

123

the picture. I had to make a fuss about something.'

'Excuse me,' said Basil, 'I know it's a silly thing to ask, but *was* that the picture you were looking for, Mrs Baynes? Things sort of blacked-out in there and I don't remember what you said.'

'It was the picture all right,' I said.

'Oh well, that's something, at any rate,' he said. 'I'm glad you got it back.'

'But who did it?' said Susan. 'Who murdered Piers?' She asked it almost in a tone of idle curiosity.

I think it was really not until that moment that I remembered Sholto and his threats against Piers in the kitchen. As I recalled them, my hand jerked and I spilled half of my drink over my skirt.

'Oh, God, you are clumsy, you're always getting yourself in a filthy mess,' said Susan automatically.

Basil produced a very clean yellow duster from his pocket and gave it to me to mop up my skirt. He really was a treasure to have around the place.

'I wonder,' I said, mopping away, while Basil refilled my glass, 'where Sholto is.'

At that moment there was a loud scream in the hall.

It turned out to have come from Mrs Fawcett, who had come out of the kitchen and had overheard Norman telling the police on the telephone that he had found a dead man in the cloakroom. Ever interested in the dead, she had gone to take a look in the cloakroom herself, and the sight had turned out to be a little more than even she could enjoy. She went on screaming until she had the whole household standing round her.

Norman's glance implored me to do something about it. Turning to Sholto, who had appeared from somewhere and was looking almost as near screaming as Mrs Fawcett, I whispered to him to stay with Susan, then I set about steering Mrs Fawcett upstairs. At first she did not want to move, but as soon as she grasped that I was saying something about her lying down, she went with surprising willingness. All the way up to her room she held tight on to my arm, and as she collapsed breathlessly on to the bed she implored me to stay with her.

'I shall die of fright if you don't, dear, I know I shall,' she said hoarsely. 'There's a murderer in the house!'

'Oh, I should think he's a long way off by now, whoever he is,' I said, 'I expect it was a burglar.'

'In broad daylight, with the house full of people? No, you and I know who it was,' she said. 'We heard him threaten this very thing. Goodness me, I never dreamt for a moment he meant it.'

'No,' I said, thinking how seldom one really
125

believed that Sholto meant what he said. He talked so much nonsense about himself that I had long ago stopped listening to him except as a mild form of amusement.

'To think that you and me sat there listening to him and giving him coffee,' she said. 'You won't leave me, will you, dear? Not till the police get here and take him away. My heart's beating so that I feel all queer.'

I took a chair and sat down. 'I ought to go back to my sister,' I said, wondering why the thought of Susan being with Sholto did not worry me. 'She's had a terrible shock.'

A cold look came into Mrs Fawcett's eyes, as if she would have liked to say that Susan deserved any shocks that were going, but she mumbled, 'Poor soul, poor soul—yes, of course you ought to be with her. But don't leave me, dear. I can't say what might happen if I was left alone, my heart's thumping so. I know you wouldn't like anything to happen.'

'I'll stay till the police get here,' I said.

I lit a cigarette. I noticed then in a detached sort of way that my hands were trembling. I felt sick too, and when I tried to remember just what I had seen in the cloakroom I felt a darkness closing in on my mind. To fight the darkness off I started looking round me. I made myself look at Mrs Fawcett's room and think about the things that were in it.

The main thing I noticed was a toilet set of magnificent silver. There were not merely

126

brushes, a comb and a mirror, but all sorts of cut-glass bottles with silver stoppers. The bottles were most of them empty, but each one stood on a separate lace doyley, and shone with the loving care it had received. I found myself thinking of a visit I had once made, as a small child, to a grand-aunt's bedroom. I had marvelled deeply even then at the scintillating display on her dressing-table, yet not as I was marvelling now. I thought how fascinating it would be to draw from Mrs Fawcett the story of her past life.

For instance, had she come of a family once rich and was this wonderful show of silver all that was left of what had once been wealth? Or had it all belonged to the wife of Mr Godstowe or Mr Daintree or one of the others, and come to her along with the little bit of money which she seemed always to obtain from these poor men in their last extremity? I thought that the more probable explanation, but it made me vaguely uncomfortable. I do not know why I never even thought that this very feminine possession could have come to her direct from a woman except that she had never mentioned working for a woman. In fact, I took for granted that she could only have obtained the silver from some widower, blinded to her faults by illness, as Norman seemed to be blinded.

At that point I breathed some smoke in the wrong way and began to choke. I choked so hard that I excused myself to Mrs Fawcett, saying that I must get a drink of water.

She immediately jumped off the bed, and followed me across the room, slammed the door shut behind me the moment I had gone out, and turned the key.

Still coughing I ran downstairs.

'Marabelle!'

I stopped. Sholto was standing at the bottom of the stairs.

'I want to talk to you,' he said in a loud whisper. His face seemed to have become even longer than usual and was grey-pale. 'I'm in a ghastly situation and you're the only person who can help me.'

Perhaps I ought to have felt fear or horror on meeting him. But the reality of the situation seemed so far to have made little impression on me. I had a habitual way of treating Sholto and I did not know how to change it.

'All right,' I said, 'let's go into the kitchen. There'll be no one there.'

'Thank you,' he said very emotionally. 'I knew I could count on you.' He went with me to the kitchen, walking with tense, abrupt little steps, holding himself unnaturally upright.

'I'll make some coffee,' I said.

'Tea,' said Sholto imploringly. 'Very strong tea. Coffee goes for my liver.'

'I didn't know you had one,' I said.

'I have when I'm upset.' He took a chair by the table while I filled the kettle. 'Marabelle, do you believe I murdered Piers?'

128

The trouble was, I did not believe it, but I felt rather guilty about this, thinking there must be something the matter with me.

He looked at me searchingly, 'You do,' he said. 'It's obvious you do. Oh God, what am I to do?'

'Well, I just don't know what I think,' I said. 'If you hadn't said all those things—'

'That's it, that's just it!' he cried. 'I'm a madman, Marabelle. Other people don't do these things, only me. Do you know any one else who'd say things like that just before a person gets murdered?'

'Well, if you didn't do it,' I said, 'the time you chose for it was just bad luck.'

'No,' he said, 'because it's the sort of thing I'm always doing, and after a bit one has to admit that it can't just be bad luck, it must be something in oneself. But I didn't do it, Marabelle, I didn't.'

'Well, I'm very glad to hear it,' I said.

'But I'm going to be arrested all the same.'

I thought about it. 'I don't think you can count on that,' I said.

'Oh yes, I can, if you tell the police what I said.'

'But wouldn't that only be hearsay or something?'

'Well, whom else will they arrest?'

'Probably no one immediately. I expect they'll go into all the evidence pretty carefully—like where we all were when it happened and so on. Where were you, Sholto?'

'I was in the garden, trying to cool off and stop thinking about Piers. I didn't know anything was up till I heard Mrs Fawcett scream.'

I noticed then that his coat was damp. So he had gone out without a mackintosh.

'Did any one see you out there?' I asked.

'I don't know. Incidentally, where were you?'

'In my bedroom, I suppose, packing.'

'Did any one see you?'

'No.'

'Good,' he said. 'The more people who were by themselves, the better.'

I thought that was not very nice of him, but too typical of him to be worth comment.

'But all the same, they'll arrest me,' he said, hitting the table before him. 'If you tell them what I said and they start thinking about my motive, they'll take me away straight off.'

'What's your motive?' I asked.

He looked at me blankly. 'You can ask that!'

'If you mean that he took your wife,' I said, 'every one knows that you were enormously relieved. I know it wouldn't have been decent to show that at the time, and I respect you very much for the appearance of outrage you managed to put up—I think it gratified Susan very much—but I don't think this is the time to make any more of it than you must.'

'So that's what you believe,' he said.

130

'Well, it was always obvious how you hated living with Susan,' I said.

'Oh yes,' he said, 'of course I did. But all the same, I was angry and humiliated beyond words when she left me. You see, I was intending to leave her. I was looking forward to it.'

'Oh ... I hadn't thought of that,' I admitted.

'I've never forgiven her,' he went on, 'and I don't suppose I ever shall. And as for Piers, I meant every single word I said about him this morning.'

'Except perhaps about actually murdering him?'

His face went a little whiter. 'God knows, perhaps I meant even that. Marabelle, do you think me an awful person?'

'Actually I've always rather liked you,' I said. 'I can't think why.'

'You have?' he said. 'You mean that? You don't hate me?'

'Oh no, I most definitely don't hate you,' I said.

'And you'd do something for me?'

'If you mean not mentioning that outburst of yours to the police,' I said, 'it wouldn't help, even if I didn't.'

'Oh, it would,' he said, 'it'd save me. It'd save my life. D'you realise that, Marabelle—my life!'

'It wouldn't,' I said, 'because Mrs Fawcett was there too—aren't you forgetting that?'

131

It looked as if he had completely forgotten it. His mouth dropped open and his eyelids flickered wildly.

'Mrs Fawcett,' he said. 'Good God, then there's no escape. None.'

I do not know what gave me the impression that he was really rather pleased, but whatever it was, the idea did not surprise me. I knew that Sholto's capacity for dramatising himself was almost without limit.

'I don't believe for a moment that they'll arrest you,' I said, 'unless they find a great deal more evidence against you.'

'Oh, they'll arrest me,' he said. 'I know now that there's no way out. But knowing it does at least solve one problem.'

'What's that,' I asked.

'What to do,' he said. 'I know now what I have to do. And that gives one peace of mind.' He gave me a sad smile. 'Anyway, thanks for listening to me. Is that tea ready yet?'

'Just about,' I said.

'I need it,' he said. 'I've been going through a terrible experience. Hope's an awful thing. One feels much better as soon as one abandons it.'

'Oh, cut it out,' I said. 'Nothing's going to happen.'

But that was where I was wrong. Sholto gave me no chance to be right. As soon as the police arrived, he gulped down the rest of his tea, choked slightly, stood up, gave his waistcoat a little tug, passed his hand over his hair, and strode out to meet them.

'Here I am,' he said. 'You had better arrest me at once for the murder of Piers Beltane.'

CHAPTER TWELVE

The inspector in charge was a large, solid sensible-looking man who faintly raised an eyebrow at Sholto, as if people who made statements of this kind were all in the day's work, and said, 'Perhaps I'd better ask a few questions before we do anything so drastic, eh?'

Sholto, of course, had known that this was the answer he would be given and he was prepared for it with some more drama. Standing very upright, as if he were a soldier being sentenced at a court-martial, he said, 'Please arrest me, Inspector, and save your questions. In the presence of two witnesses I threatened the life of Piers Beltane only a short while before he was murdered. I had a motive for murdering him and I have no alibi.'

'Ah, but did you murder him?' asked the inspector.

'No,' said Sholto, 'but it's inevitable that you should believe I did. I see that.'

The inspector began to look a trifle impatient.

Susan came forward. 'If you really saw that,'

133

she said to Sholto, 'you wouldn't be looking so pleased with yourself. Take no notice of him, Inspector, he always behaves like this.'

She introduced herself, and as if she were hostess at a party that she was giving for somebody else and in which she was not really much interested, casually introduced the rest of us. She was looking paler than usual and her eyes had sunk back into her head, but I could see no sign that she had shed any tears so far, only that there was an unusual fierceness about her. Susan was hardly ever angry and so it took me some moments to realise that she was in the grip of a violent rage.

The inspector began to ask a lot of routine questions. Who had found the body? When? How? Where? And so on. He made a long and careful examination of the body and the cloakroom. Photographs were taken. A number of men tramped to and fro, doing mysterious things. Time seemed to move very slowly while very little happened.

Yet when I happened to glance at the clock, I saw it was a quarter to one. That reminded me suddenly that Mrs Fawcett was still lying down in her bedroom and that no cooking had been done. Also I remembered that I was beginning to feel hungry, so since no one seemed to be worrying about what I did, I slipped away to the kitchen. I found Basil there, polishing the silver.

'They wouldn't let me get on with anything

else,' he said, 'so I thought I might as well do this. I like polishing silver. I like it better than anything else.'

'Well, it's wonderful to have an occupation that can comfort one in time of trouble,' I said. 'I've come to look into the question of food. I thought I might make some sandwiches or something.'

'D'you think any one will feel like eating?' said Basil. 'I know I don't.'

'My sister always feels like eating,' I said, 'particularly when she's upset. I think she'd probably like some sardines on toast.'

'That's like my brother-in-law,' said Basil. 'My sister's husband. The first thing he says when he comes into the house is "What's there to eat?" Then he kicks his shoes off in different corners of the room and throws his coat down on the floor in the middle and waits for someone else to pick them all up.'

'You don't sound fond of him.' I went to the cupboard and studied Mrs Fawcett's collection of tins. I had a curious and unfamiliar feeling that I would like to do something special for Susan, like giving her something for lunch that she would really enjoy.

'I hate him,' said Basil. 'I've been trying to drive him out of the house for months.'

'I rather took for granted that you were an only child,' I said.

'Oh no, there are seven of us,' he said, 'and

135

most of us are at home most of the time. But I'm the only one that's peculiar. For instance, I'm the only one that does a job like this.'

'I can't help wondering what made you choose it,' I said. I found it did me good to talk. I took a packet of dried egg out of the cupboard, for I had just remembered that if ever I had a meal at Susan's flat she gave me an omelette of dried egg, and from that I deduced that she must like it herself, since it did not seem to me to be in her nature to do a thing for another person from which she derived no pleasure.

Basil was rubbing ardently at a silver ash-tray. 'I sort of wonder myself,' he said. 'But I never know why I do things. I don't know why I don't—I'm just like that. For instance, I really don't know why I suddenly went and looked inside that cloakroom again after I'd finished tidying it.'

I stood still. 'You mean you tidied it and shut the door and went away, and then went back to it later on?'

'Yes,' he said, 'and I simply can't explain it, except that ... Well, you remember what I told you about turning it into a grotto?'

'Vaguely,' I said.

'Well, I was thinking about that, you see. I like thinking about things like that. And suddenly I thought I'd like to take another look at the place to make sure I had the shape of it right in my mind. I was wondering if

136

there'd be room for a palm-tree in the corner—'

'I'm sure grottos are much too cold and damp for palm trees,' I said.

'D'you think so?' He held the ash-tray so that the light from the window glinted across its brightness, and smiled at it happily. 'That makes it worse, doesn't it? I mean, the police are sure not to believe me when I tell them. I was wondering if it wouldn't be better to say that I thought I'd left a duster in there or something.'

I felt inclined to think that an imaginary palm tree in a non-existent grotto might complicate the case a good deal. 'But you'd have to be prepared to tell them where you really left the duster,' I said. 'When one starts telling lies one has to be very careful about corroborative evidence.'

'Oh, I could say I found it in my pocket,' he said. 'I'm always finding queer things there. You see, I'm always picking up oddments and putting them in my pockets, so that I can carry more things all at one time, and then I forget about them. Sometimes I even take them home and have to bring them back next day. I told Mrs Fawcett about it so that she shouldn't worry if she missed things. Once I took Mr Rice's sleeping pills home with me. That was awful, because of course he wanted them at night, and they weren't there. You see, I found them in his study, and I knew they belonged in

137

the drawer of the table beside his bed, so I popped them in my pocket, knowing I'd be starting to clean upstairs in a few minutes. And then forgot all about them ... It was really after that that Mr Rice stopped letting me go into his study.'

Something he had said had been worrying me. I knew it was something he had said before he started talking about the sleeping-pills, but I could not remember what it was. Spooning some dried egg into a basin, I said, 'I didn't know Mr Rice had to take sleeping pills...' I was interrupted by Sholto appearing. For some reason, as soon as I saw him, I knew what it was that Basil had said that had worried me. 'The picture,' I said. 'Basil, when you were tidying up the grotto, I mean the cloakroom, you didn't see the picture, did you?'

'No,' said Basil.

'When did you find it then?' I asked.

'When I went back to see about the palm tree.'

'*Palm tree?*' said Sholto, naturally enough.

Basil and I between us explained about the palm tree. Fortunately Sholto was never slow at understanding an extravagant idea.

'This is interesting,' he said when he had taken it in. He sat down and prepared to watch me getting the lunch. 'You mean that there was no picture in the cloakroom until you went in and discovered Beltane's body?'

'That's it,' said Basil.

'Just where did you find the picture?' Sholto asked.

'It was leaning against the wall, behind the door,' said Basil. 'It had its face to the wall. I think, if you look, you'll find there's—' His voice caught. 'You'll find there's blood on the back of it.'

'That's something I've been thinking about,' said Sholto. 'Blood.'

'Now for goodness sake, will you remember I'm trying to do something about some food,' I said.

But Sholto lifted his hands and looked at them carefully, as if he were some wide-awake Lady Macbeth, demonstrating the efficacy of some new, non-rationed cleansing fluid. 'The murderer ought to have plenty of blood on him,' he said. 'Unless he was wearing one of those mackintoshes that were hanging on the wall. And he could have washed his hands at the basin. But returning to the picture, d'you know I'd assumed that Piers had found the picture in the cloakroom? I've been hunting the house for the thing, looking in all sorts of unlikely places, but I can't swear to it that I ever really looked in the cloakroom. Certainly I never looked behind the door. So when Basil found the picture, I naturally supposed that Piers had found it first. But now it looks as if Piers put it there.'

'Piers or the murderer,' I said.

Sholto nodded thoughtfully. 'Yes, Piers or

the murderer. And if it was Piers...'

I had just found some wilting lettuce in the scullery, and thought I would make a salad. 'If Piers put it there,' I said, 'then it was Piers who stole it from Susan. But why on earth should he do such a thing?'

'To turn her against Norman,' said Sholto. 'You see, he not only stole the picture from Susan, but he made her think that Norman had it. Then it was probably Piers who suggested their coming down here, because that would give him a chance to plant the picture on Norman. You know,'—he began to sound excited—'I believe we've hit on something.'

I had a feeling too that perhaps we had. I was thinking of what Norman had started to tell Susan about his reason for keeping her out of the house. Sholto had not been present during that conversation, but Sholto was a person of sharp intuitions. Perhaps he already had some inkling of what had happened in London to make Norman act as strangely as he had. I wanted to ask him, but had some doubts whether or not I ought to do so with Basil present.

Sholto was going on, 'But that raises some awkward questions, doesn't it? The question of motive, to begin with. I'd a motive, of course, but leaving me out for the present, why should any one murder Piers because he was putting the Clegg in the cloakroom?'

'It could have had nothing to do with the

Clegg,' I said.

'If someone did it to get hold of the Clegg for himself,' said Sholto, 'all he had to do was wait until Piers came out again, then go in and take the picture … Oh, but I *say*—!' His voice shrilled suddenly.

'What's it now?' I asked.

'The hammer,' said Sholto. 'Where was the hammer?'

I looked at Basil. 'Where was the hammer?' I asked.

'On the shelf at the back,' he said.

Sholto did some finger exercises on the table in his excitement. 'That's what I thought. You put it there yesterday, didn't you? We all saw you.'

'Yes,' said Basil. 'It was in that box of tools I found in the cupboard.'

'You're sure about that?' said Sholto. 'I mean, the hammer was still there when you cleaned the place this morning?'

'The box was still there,' said Basil. 'I dusted the shelf and I remember sliding the box along it so that I could dust where the box had been.'

'But you can't swear that the hammer was in the box?' asked Sholto.

Basil frowned hard, staring into space. 'It was there,' he said. 'Its handle was sticking up.'

'Are you certain about that? Absolutely certain?' Sholto went on eagerly. 'Don't say so unless you are, because it's tremendously important.'

'Just why is it so important?' I asked.

'Don't you see?' said Sholto. 'The box was on a shelf at the *back* of the cloakroom. That means that the murderer must have been *inside* the cloakroom when Piers went into it, because if he'd followed him in, he'd have had to pass Piers to get to the box. Oh, but good Lord—' He stopped, staring at me in dismay.

'What's the trouble now?' I asked.

'Me,' he said.

'What's wrong with you?'

'Don't you see, it's another nail in my coffin? Because why should any one have been in that cloakroom—I mean, what does one go into cloakrooms for?'

'I don't know,' I said. 'What does one?'

'To take off a coat, of course—or put one on.'

'And why does that incriminate you—except that you like having people think about you all the time?'

'Because I ought to have gone into the cloakroom to put on a coat before going out to walk in the rain, and then I ought to have come in again and gone into the cloakroom to take my coat off again. And I could have been doing that, and the police are sure to think I actually was doing it, when Piers went into the cloakroom.'

'But you didn't put a coat on, did you?' I said. 'Your jacket's damp.'

'But that's suspicious in itself. I might have been in the cloakroom wearing my coat when Piers came in. Then I should have had to go out without a coat, because of having got it splashed with blood.'

'Norman also went out into the garden,' I said.

As I said it, I realised with horror how easy it might be to make out a case against Norman. For it was Norman who had the best motive.

Basil picked up a silver soup-ladle and began to smear it with plate-powder. 'It sounds to me,' he said, 'as if this murderer is awfully like my brother-in-law.'

'What d'you mean by that?' asked Sholto.

'Impulsive,' said Basil. 'Just think, he goes into the cloakroom to take off his coat or put it on, then another man comes into the cloakroom and so the first man picks up a hammer and hits the second man on the head. He can't have thought it out, because if he had he'd have been careful not to have a reason, like wanting to take off his coat, for being in the cloakroom at all. In fact,' he added with a sweet smile at Sholto, 'I'd say your idea was all nonsense except that that's just the sort of thing my brother-in-law would do. He's an awful man.'

'Perhaps it *was* your brother-in-law,' I said.

Sholto was looking at Basil with an interest he had not shown before. 'You know, what you've just said is very important,' he said. 'I

143

was being a fool. Of course the significant point is, not that the murderer was taking off his coat, but that he knew that Piers was going to take off his coat. He knew that if he waited in the cloakroom, Piers would come in sooner or later and could be hit over the head with the hammer.'

'Suppose Piers hadn't come in,' I said.

'Then there'd have been no harm done. When the murderer got tired of waiting, he could simply have come out again and waited for another opportunity.'

'And suppose someone else had come in instead of Piers?'

'There's a basin in there—he could have been washing his hands. But, of course, this may be all wrong, because there's another possibility...' Sholto paused, rubbing his long chin. 'I don't think it's a nice possibility.'

'I don't really see how niceness comes into the situation at all,' I said.

'Well, some ideas are definitely worse than others.'

'Tell us the worst,' I said.

'I was just thinking,' said Sholto, 'suppose it was an impulsive murder, a more or less accidental murder...'

'I don't see why that makes it worse,' I said.

He gave me a curious look, doing some more finger exercises the table. I felt that I was being stupid and missing some obvious point. Sholto's face had developed a look of keenness

144

that I could not remember having seen on it before. I remembered that Susan had always insisted that he was very intelligent and that I had always refused to see this. Now I began to feel that Susan could have been right.

'Why does it make it worse?' I repeated, feeling a new stirring of anxiety.

He was just starting to reply when Susan walked into the kitchen.

She looked round at my preparations for lunch and said, 'How much longer before we get something to eat? I'm ravenous.'

Sholto jumped to his feet. 'If you say that sort of thing in front of the inspector,' he said wildly, 'he'll decide at once you're the murderer. No woman of decent feeling would be feeling hungry when her husband's just been murdered—and when both her former husbands are liable to be under suspicion.'

I said, 'Sit down, Sholto. You seem to think the inspector forms his opinions as emotionally as you do yours.'

'Well, I *am* ravenous,' said Susan, picking a piece of lettuce out of the bowl where I had put it ready for the dressing. 'How long before we can eat?'

The trouble was, my preparations for lunch had somehow been becoming more complicated while we were talking. I had found some whites of eggs in a cup in the larder and I had felt that I could not bear not to use them, so I had started making a Queen of Puddings.

145

'Don't fuss,' I said. 'You'll get something sooner or later.'

'I must have something now or I shall die,' said Susan. 'Isn't there some cheese or something?'

I left her to scrounge for herself, and went on with what I was doing. She found the remains of a custard pudding in the larder and settled down to eat it straight out of the glass bowl.

'So Norman had the picture all the time,' she said. 'D'you know, I never knew he could be such a liar? When he told me straight out he hadn't got it and then said why it was he wouldn't let me come here, I simply believed him. It's given me a frightful shock, finding out that he could make up a thing like that. Such a rotten thing to make up too.'

Sholto asked her what she meant.

'Haven't you told him?' she asked me.

I shook my head.

'Well, just before Basil came in and told us about finding Piers,' said Susan, 'Norman had had the kindness to tell me that the reason he wouldn't let me come here any more was that my husband had been making love to my daughter. He also swore solemnly that he hadn't got my Clegg. Then Basil walked in with it—'

'But Susan,' I said, 'it really looks as if Norman didn't have the picture.'

'He must have had it,' she said, 'and it's obvious what happened. He and Piers met outside the house this morning, both with their raincoats on, and then Norman lured Piers into the cloakroom and killed him. D'you know that Norman's raincoat is all over blood?'

I felt a sudden violent aversion to the pudding I was making, but I conquered it and started beating the whites of eggs. I knew that eventually, when it was cooked, Susan would enjoy it.

'We've been talking about that,' said Sholto, 'and it doesn't mean anything. But the thing about the picture is that probably it was Piers who put it into the cloakroom, because it wasn't there when Basil did the place out earlier in the morning—'

A movement in the doorway checked him. The inspector stood there. He was looking at Susan, as she sat with her legs crossed, spooning down her custard-pudding. The expression on his face was one which I recognised from long practice as intense admiration. But his voice was level and toneless when he spoke. 'I heard you talking about that picture,' he said. 'Do you happen to be aware that it's gone missing again?'

CHAPTER THIRTEEN

Susan's spoon hit her plate with a clatter. She gave a shudder and said, 'No, I don't believe it. I don't believe any of it!'

I had an idea of what was happening in her mind. She believed that Norman had stolen the picture once already, she believed that he had murdered Piers, she believed that he had now stolen the picture a second time. But she could not bear to believe all three things at the same time. That was too much for her. So she made a general declaration of disbelief in everything.

'Well, it's gone,' said the inspector, 'and Mr Rice says he doesn't know what's become of it.'

Susan shook her head. 'No,' she said, 'at least he wouldn't do *that*.'

'Who?' asked the inspector.

'Norman.'

'Wouldn't do what?'

She shook her head again and did not answer.

He said patiently, still looking at her, 'I'm curious about this picture.'

Sholto and I both began to speak at the same time, and both stopped.

The inspector looked at me. 'I think I'd like a word with you, Mrs Baynes. Will you come into the study, please.'

Looking at my preparations for lunch, I said

regretfully, 'I wonder when we'll get around to eating this meal.' I was beginning to feel almost as hungry as Susan generally was, but I wiped my hands and went along with the inspector to Norman's study.

As I went into it, I looked at the desk, where Basil had put the picture before he fainted, and certainly there was no picture there now, while some papers, which I remembered as having been in a fairly neat pile on the desk, were spread out and half of them tumbled on to the floor.

The inspector closed the door. There was another man in plain clothes in the room. He pushed a chair forward for me, then as the inspector also sat down, took up a place behind him, leaning against a tall bookcase.

'As I said,' said the inspector, 'I'm curious about that picture.'

'When did it disappear again?' I asked.

'I'm hoping someone else can tell me that,' he said.

'The last time I saw it,' I said, 'it was here on the desk. Basil put it there when he came in to tell us about finding Mr Beltane's body.'

'Just when was this last time that you saw it?' he asked.

'Then,' I said, 'when Basil put it there.'

'But didn't you come back into this room later?'

'No.'

'Not once?'

149

'No.'

I did not understand the look he gave me. It was as if he felt he had a good reason for disbelieving me. Gesturing at the papers on the desk and the floor, he went on, 'Do you remember anything of the position of these before the picture was put down on them?'

'They were in a pile,' I said.

'On the desk?'

'Just there.' I pointed.

'So it looks as if they got upset when the picture was lifted off them?' he suggested.

'That's how it looks,' I said.

'You weren't here when it happened?'

'No.'

'You're telling me you left this room as soon as the boy came in and told you what he had found, and that you did not come back at all until you came in here with me just now?'

'Yes,' I said, beginning to feel agitated by his persistence, 'that's how it happened.'

His next remark suggested to me that his mind was not really on his job and that he was merely talking to fill in time for some mysterious purpose of his own. 'That's a very nice rose you're wearing,' he said.

'It is,' I agreed.

'But about this picture,' he said, 'isn't it a fact that you came down here expressly to get it?'

'Are you suggesting,' I asked, 'that I've got it hidden somewhere now?'

'If you don't mind,' he said, 'I'll ask the questions.'

I have never seen why this particular retort should silence any one. I said, 'Well, what are you suggesting?'

He shook his head. 'Various people have told me some bits and pieces of a story from which I've only succeeded in arriving at a very confused notion of what actually took place. I'd like your version of the story too.'

So I told him everything that had happened from the time of Susan's coming to see me on Sunday morning. That is to say, I told him everything that seemed to me of importance. I did not consciously omit anything that I thought could possibly be relevant to Piers' death or to the mysterious wanderings of the picture, and I did not intentionally distort anything. Whether or not the impression of what had happened that I managed to convey to the inspector was anywhere near the truth, I had, of course, no means of knowing. I had a good deal of difficulty in getting him to understand the relationship between Susan, Piers, Sholto and Norman, and by the time I had finished I was so hungry that I would have eaten one of Mrs Fawcett's meals with the greatest thankfulness.

Remembering Mrs Fawcett, I wondered how she was getting on upstairs in her locked room, and asked the inspector if he had seen her yet.

151

He said absently, 'Mrs Fawcett? Oh yes, the housekeeper. No, I'll get around to her presently. D'you expect her to have anything particular to tell me?'

'No,' I said, 'except that if that picture was in this house before Mr Beltane got here, she might have seen it.'

The inspector gave me a sharp look. '*Before* Mr Beltane got here? You're implying that he might have brought it?'

I felt that I was unfairly stealing Sholto's thunder, but that having started this, I might as well go on. So I told him again of Basil's certainty that the picture had not been in the cloakroom when he cleaned it, and I underlined what this might mean.

'Oh, yes,' he said, sounding once more as if his mind were wandering. I wondered if he had worries at home. 'Now about that nice rose you're wearing...'

As he paused I felt a pang of fear which I could not explain but which was very unpleasant. My hand went to the rose. I began to unpin it.

'No,' said the inspector, 'I don't want it. I merely think it's a little curious, if you really haven't been in here since the time when the picture was put down on this desk, that there should have been rose-petals mixed up with the papers on the floor?'

So this was what he had really brought me here to tell me. All the time that I had been telling him what I knew, this was what he had been saving up for me.

With the rose in one hand and the pin in the other, I looked at him stupidly while I tried to think out what rose-petals on the study floor could mean. To give myself more time, because I have never been good at thinking quickly, I carefully pinned the rose into my buttonhole again.

'Are you sure they were from this rose?' I asked.

'From a rose of that colour,' he said.

'There's usually more than one rose on a bush,' I said.

'Quite so, but there seems to be only one rose of that colour in this house at the moment.'

'You've looked in the garden?'

'There are no roses in bloom in the garden.'

I do not know why I did not tell him that the rose was one of Ernst Weinkraut's. I was in a muddle, trying to think out if it was conceivable that Ernst or Millie had come into the room while every one else was gathered round the body of Piers Beltane, and had removed the Roger Clegg. For that, I could see, was what must have happened, even if it was not wholly thinkable. Either Ernst or Millie could have stepped in at the window, as I had the evening before, quickly taken the picture, dropping a few rose-petals and scattering the papers, and then gone out by the window again, possibly without even knowing of the calamity in the house.

But if that was what had happened, they would be thinking now that the presence of the police here was on account of the theft, and realising that, I thought that at the first opportunity I would run over and reassure them. I had become so used to suspecting all sorts of unlikely people of being capable of stealing a moderately valuable picture, that I had stopped thinking of it as anything to worry about, and I hated the thought that Ernst or Millie should be sitting in the bungalow, imagining that the police were after them.

Probably it was confused feelings of this sort that stopped me telling the inspector how I had come by the rose, and this, I heard later, made him suspect for a time that I was having an affair with Ernst, and that I might have murdered Piers to stop him revealing the fact to Millie. This suspicion was strengthened when Sholto told him that I had recently been deserted by my husband, who had gone off to Bermuda with a half-caste woman.

Seeing that he had come to the end of the information that I could or would give him, the inspector let me go. Hurrying back to the kitchen, I began again on cooking the lunch, but I could see that it would be at least three o'clock before it was ready. Unfortunately I could not stop thinking about the rose-petals in the study, and how I was to convey a warning to Millie and Ernst, and so I kept spilling things and mislaying things and letting things boil over.

The kitchen had been empty when I first returned to it, but Sholto soon scented me out and came and sat down at the table again, rather in my way. He was calmer now but extremely serious.

'Marabelle, I've been doing some more thinking,' he said. 'I've realised something that's making me feel very uncomfortable.'

'If you think you're under suspicion,' I said, 'I shouldn't worry. I've a sort of feeling that I'm suspect number one.'

'Oh, I'm not worrying about myself,' he said. 'I'm developing a theory, and I don't like it. I can't exactly say why I dislike it so much, except that there's something unfinished about it. It gives me a sort of feeling of foreboding. Would you like me to tell you about it?'

'Yes,' I said, 'you'd better.'

'Well, you remember what I said about Piers having the picture all the time, and taking it to the cloakroom to plant it there to make trouble for Norman? I believe that's what happened. It seems to me to make sense. But that brings us around to the question of motive. Did the picture have anything to do with it? Because, you see, the murderer must have been in the cloakroom already when Piers came in. We've agreed about that, haven't we, because of the position of the box of tools? If the picture is really anything but an accidental

155

complication, the murderer must have known that Piers was just about to bring the picture to the cloakroom. And the only person, if you come to think of it, who could really have known that Piers had the picture all the time, and was going to put it in the cloakroom, is Susan.'

'Stop!' I exclaimed. 'Susan didn't do this.'

'I'm not suggesting it,' he said. 'I'm only showing you the logical end to a certain line of conjecture. Let's go on to considering what must have happened if the murder had nothing to do with the picture. In that case, the murderer was in the cloakroom, either lying in wait for Piers, or—not lying in wait for him.' He dropped his voice on the last few words and gave me a very strange look.

I said, 'I don't get it.'

'But don't you see? If the murderer was waiting for Piers, then it must have been someone who knew he'd gone out for a walk, wearing a coat which he would shortly be returning to the cloakroom. That might have been any of us, and probably it was one of us, and Norman seems the likeliest, because he had the most reason to hate Piers—or me, of course. I'd a pretty good reason. But now suppose the other thing...' He made another of his significant pauses.

'I still don't get it,' I said. But that was largely out of stubbornness, because the idea he was trying to convey to me was beginning to

156

emerge cloudily in my mind.

Sholto put all his finger tips on the table and leant upon them. I could see that it was a really big rabbit that he was going to take out of his hat.

'If the murderer was not waiting for Piers,' he said, 'and that's logically perfectly possible and so must be considered, and if all the same he found it necessary or desirable to murder Piers, then it must have been because Piers discovered him in some act which it would have been disastrous in the extreme to the murderer to have known. So disastrous as actually to precipitate murder.'

'But what?' I said.

'Suppose,' said Sholto, 'that the murderer was simply *hiding* in the cloakroom.'

'But in that case—'

'In that case,' said Sholto, who did not want me to have any share in his ideas, 'in that case, someone was in this house, hiding in the cloakroom, who objected very deeply to having his presence here known by any one else. And that's what I don't like to think about, Marabelle. That's what I find very nasty indeed. Because if there was someone unknown here in this house this morning, who would do a murder to stop being discovered, then he was here for a purpose, wasn't he? Some pretty sinister purpose. *And we don't know what it was.*'

CHAPTER FOURTEEN

'If, if, if,' I said.

But as if a scene in colour had been suddenly projected on the wall before me, I saw papers on a carpet and rose-petals scattered over the papers. Contemplation of it made me feel dizzy. I had always been very fond of Ernst and Millie and I could not bear to think the thoughts about them that I was thinking then.

Sholto noticed nothing wrong and went on talking. I did not listen and after a moment told him to move so that I could lay the table. I had decided to make people eat in the kitchen, because one seemed to see fewer policemen there than in the rest of the house.

As I had expected, it was past three o'clock when we at last began to eat. I did not offer to feed the policemen, but Susan, who was beginning to form a friendly relationship with the inspector, insisted on providing coffee. Basil took a tray up to Mrs Fawcett, and reported, on returning, that she had got into bed, wrapped a shawl round her head and had informed him of her intention to stay there the rest of the day.

I happened to be facing the fireplace when he told us of this, with the photographs of Mr Daintree, Mr Godstowe and Mr Pertwee looking solemnly down at me, and all of a sudden it seemed to me completely obvious that Mrs Fawcett had murdered them all. I felt that I had known since the first time I had met her that the little woman was a poisoner.

But at that point I managed to collect my wits and reminded myself that Piers had not been poisoned, but had been killed by some very heavy blows with a hammer, and that although he was a small man, the one person in the house who was smaller still was Mrs Fawcett.

The meal steadied my imagination a little. Afterwards Basil and I did the washing-up, while Susan returned to her work on the inspector. I did not know if she had any particular aim in view or if it was automatic. Basil told me that as soon as the washing-up was done he was going home. It was his usual time for leaving, and the police had said they did not need him on the premises. He had another client, he explained, in the afternoon, but he would come back later if he could help. I told him I thought that we could manage. Then I had an idea. I realised that I should probably have to stay here for some time, and that even if Mrs Fawcett insisted on staying in bed, I was going to have some difficulty in keeping my thoughts occupied.

'Are you going anywhere near the shops?' I asked.

Basil said he was.

So I asked him to buy me some paint, some

brushes and some turpentine.

'What colour paint?' asked Basil.

In ordinary circumstances I should never have dreamt of leaving such a choice to him, but as things were I had to trust him.

'A nice sort of egg-shell blue,' I said, 'or the nearest thing to it.'

His face lit up with enthusiasm. 'That sounds lovely,' he said, 'it's one of my favourite colours. What are you going to paint?'

'I'm not quite sure,' I said, 'but I'll find something.'

He seemed really to enjoy the thought of buying the paint, and hurried off all the faster to see to it, saying he would deliver it that evening after he had finished with his other client.

When he had gone, I sat down in the kitchen and thought what a relief it felt to be alone. I remember I wondered how much it would cost and how long it would take to telephone to Holland, but since I had not really the faintest idea where John would be in the middle of the afternoon, I gave up the idea, deciding instead to consult Norman about sending a cable. Not that there was anything that John could do if he came back, and he was probably enjoying his conference.

All the same, when I had had a little while of sitting quietly by myself, I went looking for Norman. I found him upstairs in his bedroom, lying down. Seeing how ill he looked, I was going to leave again, when he called me in. 'I wanted a chance to talk to you,' he said. 'Come in and shut the door.'

'You're looking pretty bad,' I said. 'What *is* the trouble, Norman?'

'Nothing to worry about,' he said. 'Snow talks nonsense about an ulcer, and says I'll have to have it operated. All nonsense, and anyway I didn't want to be stuck away in hospital while this trouble with Piers and Beryl was on.'

'When did it begin—the ulcer, I mean?' I asked.

'I had the first attack of pain about a month ago,' he said. 'But let's not talk about it. I believe myself these things are mostly nervous. I wanted to talk to you about something else.'

'Susan?' I asked.

He nodded.

I took a chair and brought it near to the bed, sitting down and lighting a cigarette.

'What d'you think will happen to her now?' he asked.

'She'll probably marry that inspector,' I said.

'No, I'm serious.'

'So am I.'

'But he's married already, I believe.'

'A minor impediment.'

'I was wondering…' He paused, and I thought I knew what he was going to say, but I was wrong. 'D'you think there's any chance

161

that she'll go back to Sholto?'

'That hadn't even occurred to me,' I said.

'But mightn't she, all the same?'

I thought it over. 'I don't think so,' I said. 'For one thing, I don't believe he'd have it. I believe you might let her come back to you, if she wanted to, but I don't believe Sholto would.'

'No, I'm afraid you're wrong,' he said. 'I wouldn't have Susan back for anything on earth.' He gave a smile. 'I've had relative peace for a number of years, and I rather like it. Susan takes it out of one. But I'm surprised at what you say about Sholto. He told me himself yesterday that he was as much in love with her as ever.'

I looked around for an ash-tray. 'D'you know. I've a feeling you're being guileful about something,' I said. 'Are you by any chance fishing around to see if I think Sholto had a motive for murdering Piers?'

'Perhaps, incidentally,' he admitted. 'And I gather that you don't think he had.'

'Well, he hated Piers,' I said. 'He was saying so himself, with decorations, only a little while before the murder. But I don't think I'd take Sholto's hates or loves very seriously.'

'You could be wrong,' he said.

'Yes . . . But is Sholto the person you suspect, Norman?'

'I think if I were any one but myself,' he said, 'I should suspect myself. I'm really the one

162

person in the house with a good motive. I was afraid Piers was going to set about ruining my daughter's life. But after me, the next suspect is Sholto, don't you think? I dare say his hates and his loves aren't very powerful, but that might make his capacity for envy and jealousy all the more terrible.'

'He himself thinks the murder was done by someone whom we didn't know was in the house,' I said. 'And that reminds me...'

But Norman took me up quickly on the first part of what I had said. 'Someone not in the house? How did he arrive at that?'

I explained Sholto's theory to him.

While I was speaking, the hard lines of a frown appeared across Norman's forehead. 'That's the first thing I've heard that's made me seriously begin to suspect Sholto,' he said. 'It's so far-fetched, it makes one wonder what he's trying to put over.'

'I'm not sure—I had a feeling there might be something in it,' I said uneasily.

'But what could this mysterious person be doing in the house?'

'Well, I was wondering if you could tell me anything about that.'

'Why I?'

'Because you know what's been going on in the house... Norman, d'you mind if I ask you something?'

'No, go on.'

'How do you and Ernst get on these days?'

He gave an impatient laugh. 'You aren't suspecting Ernst, are you? He's almost certainly got a complete alibi.'

'All the same, I wish you'd answer my question.'

'We get on excellently,' he said. 'Besides, are you forgetting, it was Piers who was murdered, not me?'

'No, but...' I knew I was becoming confused. 'You don't know if he's been up to anything odd recently that might—well, make him come into this house secretly.'

'There's nothing that I know of,' said Norman. 'But why are you suspicious of Ernst?'

I could have told him about the rose-petals but he looked as if he were in pain, and I did not want to add more worries or perplexities to his thoughts.

'It's only because Sholto had this idea of an outsider having done the murder,' I said. 'D'you agree with Sholto that Piers must have had the picture all the time?'

'Yes,' said Norman, 'I'm sure he's right there. Piers must have taken it and hidden it and then put it into Susan's head that it was I who'd stolen it, simply to make her force an entry here, so that he could see more of Beryl. But there's something I still can't understand, and that's where Sholto comes in? What's he really doing here, Marabelle?'

'He came to get the picture.'

'For Susan?'

'That's what he says. She says no.'

'What d'you think?'

'I really don't know. Susan thinks he was trying to get hold of the picture just to annoy her, or to get something out of her—or that's what she says she thinks.'

'Have you got your doubts?'

'I always have doubts where she's concerned.'

'In any case, if that's the way she speaks of him, it doesn't sound as if she'll consider going back to him.' There was a surprising note of melancholy in Norman's voice.

'But why d'you want her to?' I asked.

'Well, perhaps it's to save myself the trouble of getting acquainted with yet another husband-in-law, or whatever the relationship is,' said Norman. 'I rather recoil from the thought of going through it all again. Yet I'm sure I shall have to.'

'But I shouldn't think the inspector will want that,' I said. 'I should think he's the strong-minded type that believes in a complete break with the past.'

Norman smiled. 'Apart from that,' he said, 'I think getting married again would do Sholto good. He needs someone to keep pushing at him, then I think he might make something of himself. He has an excellent mind when he troubles to use it. And Beryl and Maurice are used to him and like him.'

It astonished me that he should think that Maurice and Beryl liked Sholto. I was quite sure that they did not, and never had, and never would.

'Sholto's vaguely thinking of marrying various other people,' I said, 'and I'm sure Susan's got no use for him any more.'

'I might be able to influence the situation a little,' said Norman thoughtfully. 'I must think it out. A new will might help ... Yes, I'll think about that.'

It sounded fantastic. Illness or anxiety, I thought, must be doing strange things to Norman's mind. But what he had said had reminded me of something and I bounced forward in my chair. 'I'd been meaning to ask you something,' I said. 'Don't think I'm crazy, but it's something I really want to know. Have you left any money to Mrs Fawcett in your will?'

'Of course not,' he said. 'She's only been here a short time.'

'Does she know you haven't?'

'She's got no reason to suppose that I have.' He looked at me in surprise. 'It hadn't occurred to me to discuss the matter with her.'

'No,' I said. 'I see. Stupid of me. Sorry. All the same ...'

'Yes?'

'I wish you'd just drop a casual remark in her hearing that you aren't leaving her anything.'

'I can't possibly do such a thing. It would be

166

insulting.'

'Yes, I know. But still ... You see, all the old gentlemen she's worked for seem to have left her a little bit of money, and—and they all die, Norman!'

'Well, naturally it's only from the ones who died that she inherited anything,' he said laughing. 'And naturally too they're much more interesting than the ones who went on living and gave her notice, and so she talks about them more. Calm down, Marabelle. You're letting things get on top of you.'

'I suppose I am.' Apologising, I got up and went out, hearing another amused laugh from Norman as I went.

I went along the passage. I turned towards the stairs. Someone who was coming up reached the top at just the same moment as I did. It was Beryl. She was wearing her gardening clothes, breeches, a check shirt and an old corduroy jacket. I stared at her. Pinned to the lapel of the jacket was a wilting yellow rose.

CHAPTER FIFTEEN

Taking a swift look past her into the hall below I saw that there was nobody there. Gripping her by the elbow, I asked in a sharp whisper, 'Has any one seen you?'

'No,' she said, wonderingly.

'Then give me that rose.'

I said it with such decision that she had unpinned it and given it to me before it had occurred to her to ask me why I wanted it. I put it in my pocket.

'Come into my room,' I said. 'I want to talk to you.'

Still saying nothing she went with me. She was very pale and her eyes were frightened.

'I suppose you've heard the news?' I said as I shut the door upon us.

She nodded, swallowing. She was having trouble with tears.

'How did you hear?' I asked.

'Mummy rang up,' she said. 'I came as quickly as I could.'

'When did she ring up?'

'During the lunch-hour. She spoke to Mr Foster and he came and told me.'

'How far away is this place where you work?'

'About two miles.'

'And you cycled?'

'Yes.'

'It's taken you rather a long time to get here, hasn't it?'

'Mr Foster didn't tell me straight away. But why d'you want to know? I don't understand.'

'What d'you mean, he didn't tell you straight away?'

'Well, he—he couldn't find me.'

'Why not?'

'Because I—I'd taken my lunch somewhere else. But please, Marabelle—'

'Where had you taken your lunch?'

'To the pub, if you must know.' She was still child enough to answer almost automatically any string of questions fired at her with sufficient authority. 'I went there with a man I know. He's Tom—Mr Foster's foreman—and he's very nice. As a matter of fact, he's one of the nicest people I've ever met. And so when he asked me if I'd like to have a glass of beer with my sandwiches, I said, yes please, and then—well, we got talking, and we stayed on later than we should have done.'

'Good,' I said. 'That sounds fine. And now tell me, how did you get that rose?'

Her eyes focused suddenly on the rose in my buttonhole. 'You aren't jealous, are you, Marabelle? I got it from Ernst, of course—as you must have got yours.'

'When did you see Ernst?'

'This morning, when I was starting out to work. I met him in the garden.'

'He was up early then.'

'He always gets up very early and does some gardening before he goes off to the Observatory,' she said. 'This morning he was coming over to put two roses on the kitchen window-sill for you. But when he met me he gave me one of them and insisted on my wearing it. You know what he's like.'

'Yes,' I said, feeling relieved. I did not see

169

how Beryl could have shed rose-petals in the study at the significant time. I hoped Mr Foster's foreman was as nice as she thought he was. 'I'm sorry I've hurled all these questions at you, but really it was important, and if I were you I shouldn't say anything about the rose. It'll save you some bother and a lot of explaining.'

She shrugged her shoulders. The rose was not important to her since it had not been given to her by Mr Foster's foreman. But now, as my questions stopped and she had time to think again, the look of fear came back into her eyes.

'Marabelle, it is true, is it—that Sholto's murdered Piers?'

'Is that what Susan told you?'

'Well, no. She told me it's what the police think—and it's what I've been hoping, all the way home.'

'Is there something attractive about the idea?' I was interested.

'Well, don't you see,' she said, 'if Sholto did it, then I'm not to blame. Sholto had no reason to murder Piers because of me. But if Mummy or Daddy did it—'

She stopped, looking at me with haggard misery in her face.

I saw what she meant and nodded.

Abruptly she began to cry. It began without any preliminary swimming of the eyes or half-resisted sobs. Dropping into a chair, she bent her head into her hands and wept with complete abandonment.

It was some minutes before she began to talk again. Her voice was low and rough with tears. 'I didn't understand what I was doing,' she said. 'I never thought. I've never taken Piers seriously as Mummy's husband. I suppose I didn't even like him much. Then I got awfully excited and lost my head, and I suppose I made much more of it than I should have, because really nothing happened except a lot of talk from Piers. And when I got home again I couldn't sort it out, and I got depressed and angry with everybody, and I let Daddy know what had happened. That's where I'm to blame. I know I ought to have said nothing about it. But I'm not used to keeping things to myself. I always tell things to Daddy and Maurice.'

As soon as she had said it she immediately broke into violent weeping again. I did not think of trying to stop her. It always seems to me a good idea to cry when one wants to.

'You don't think it was Mummy or Daddy, do you?' she managed to ask after a minute.

'Certainly not,' I said, putting all the firmness I possessed into my voice.

'Then who do you think it was?'

'I haven't the faintest idea,' I said.

'Do you think it was Sholto?'

'I wish I could make up my mind,' I said.

'It must have been Sholto, mustn't it?'

'Why?' I was curious to know her honest

opinion of her various stepfathers.

'Because he always hated Piers,' she said. 'He hates Mummy too. I can't put it very well, but I always feel that Sholto—well, he's never really had anything much in his life, anything really his own, as Piers had his painting, and Mummy has her beauty, and Daddy has— well, his own self, so to speak? And so it's easier to humiliate Sholto than most people, and he worries more about it.'

'All the same, I'd sooner not leap to any conclusions yet. Sholto himself says there must have been someone in the house whom none of us knew was there.'

She looked up sharply, brushing her tears away. I was astonished at the change that had come over her face. If I had thought about it, I should have expected relief. Generally, when I wanted to cheer myself up, I returned to this theory of Sholto's and thought how comforting it was. But the look I saw in Beryl's eyes, after the first momentary blankness, was blind terror. All colour, except from her reddened eyelids, had drained out of her face. Then, as she began to get command of herself again after this profound shock that I appeared to have given her, she lost her temper with me.

She jumped to her feet. 'That can't be true— it's nonsense, stupid nonsense. Why are you trying to twist things like that? Isn't it obvious Sholto did it. I'm going to the police and I'm going to tell them so.'

'I shouldn't do that,' I said.

'I will. It can't be any one but Sholto. And if he's telling people a story like that, then I know it was him.' Her voice was thin with hysteria. 'It's just like him to lie in wait in a cloakroom and kill somebody. When we were little and he first came here to visit Daddy—before he married Mummy—he used to hide behind doors and jump out at Maurice and me and say boo!'

'He probably thought it would amuse you,' I said.

'He didn't, he wanted to frighten us.'

'He hates it if one does anything like that to him,' I said reflectively. 'Still I shouldn't go to the police till they want you. And then I'd just tell them facts.'

'That's a fact, about his hiding behind doors.'

I thought suddenly of Sholto climbing in at a window at dead of night to steal a picture. Perhaps hiding behind doors to jump out and say boo did belong to the same character. And perhaps hiding in cloakrooms with intent to murder might be a maturer expression of the same tendency. But I wanted to know what had brought on this explosion.

'Why don't you like the idea of the murderer being some outsider, a tramp, for instance?'

She gave me a contemptuous stare. 'That isn't what he meant—and you know it.' Before

I could ask her another question she spun on her heel and ran out of the room. When I went to the door to see where she was going, I was just in time to see the door of her bedroom closing and to hear the key turning in the lock.

The sound reminded me of Mrs Fawcett, locked into her room upstairs, and that reminded me of dinner. It was not too early to start cooking, and would be pleasanter to cook than to sit and think. So I went down to the kitchen again and began another search for food.

While I was at it, Basil blew in at the door, fresh as an evening breeze. He had bought paint, brushes and turpentine. The sight of them cheered me up a good deal, and when I found a cache of rice and some tomatoes and anchovies and some tinned peas, I thought we need not do so badly, and set about producing a rather individual kind of *pilaff*, which I thought that I myself would enjoy, even if nobody else did.

In fact everybody seemed to like it except Mrs Fawcett, who said, when I took some up on a tray, that somehow she couldn't fancy it and might she have just a cup of hot milk instead? She gave me careful instructions.

'Not the milk bottle with the gold top, dear—that's Mr Rice's T.T. milk—oh, and that reminds me! His hot milk at night! You'll see to that, won't you, dear? The doctor says he must have it to soothe his nerves. He's been

174

sleeping ever so much better since he's been having it, and not taking nearly so many of those pills. Nasty things, pills—I don't hold with them. You will remember, won't you? He's so considerate, he'll never ask for it if you don't.'

I promised her that I would and went down again to get the hot milk she wanted.

I was just beginning on this when Susan unexpectedly turned helpful.

'You sit down and eat and I'll see to it,' she said. 'It's a shame, the way we've been letting you do everything.'

Naturally I seized the opportunity to make a martyred face and to say in a resigned voice, 'Oh, I'm glad to help in any way I can.'

'Like hell you are,' said Susan, going to the refrigerator. 'You've been looking poison at everybody all the time.'

'I'm afraid that's just my natural face,' I said. 'When I was a child people called it pensive. Now they call it worse things—hi, stop!' For Susan had just taken from the refrigerator the milk bottle with the gilt top and had already driven her thumb-nail through the thin metal cap and half-levered it off. 'That's Norman's special milk,' I said. 'Mrs Fawcett gets common-or-garden milk with a silver top.'

Susan returned the bottle of T.T. milk to the refrigerator and took out a bottle of the ordinary pasteurised milk. She heated it, put it

175

in a mug, then sent Beryl up with it to Mrs Fawcett.

Beryl had been completely silent since she had come down to dinner, and had a set, sullen look on her face. She refused to meet my eyes and if Sholto came anywhere near her, she immediately moved away. The meal was a rather horrible affair, with Norman hardly eating anything and looking lost in some strange dream, and Susan and Sholto being snappishly unpleasant to one another.

I always hate washing-up at night even more than at any other time of the day, and that evening I was more disinclined to it than usual. So when no one else volunteered to do the job, I simply left the debris where it was, thinking that if I did not come down too early to breakfast next day, Basil, being a nice boy, would get on with it.

But I loitered in the kitchen, smoking, until every one had gone, then I switched out the light, went to the back door and opened it softly. For a minute or two I stood in the doorway, listening, and could hear no sounds in the garden except the soft rustle of leaf against leaf. After a moment, closing the door quietly, I walked quickly across the garden to the Weinkrauts'.

Though the curtains were drawn, I could see there were lights in the sitting-room. Yet when I rang, it was a surprisingly long time before there were any sounds in the bungalow. I had a

176

feeling, in fact, that some sound had been silenced by the ringing of the bell. At last, however, I heard footsteps inside, the door opened a few inches and Ernst's spectacles peered at me though the crack.

'Marabelle!' His tone was one of relief. 'Come in, come in quickly!' Catching my arm, he hustled me inside. 'Thank God you have come!'

'Whom were you expecting?' I asked.

Millie's grey, untidy head appeared round the sitting room door. 'We didn't know who it mightn't be,' she said. 'A perfectly frightful thing's happened.'

'It was very lucky you came,' said Ernst. 'We have been praying for it.'

It is the only time to my knowledge that my coming anywhere has been prayed for. It gave me a disturbing feeling of responsibility.

'Then you know what's happened to Piers?' I said.

'Piers?' they said together.

I was thrust into the sitting-room and the door was quickly and furtively closed, as if there were enemies outside.

'Then you don't know,' I said. As a matter of fact, I had thought it strange that if they knew, neither of them had been over to offer sympathy and cups of tea.

'We only know about the picture,' said Ernst, 'and the trouble is, we don't know about that any more.'

'Well, Piers was murdered this morning,' I said. 'We found his body in the grotto, I mean the cloakroom, and nobody knows who's done it.'

This produced complete silence. They did not look at me, but at one another. I went on and told them most of what had happened, meaning to arrive eventually at the rose-petals amongst Norman's scattered papers. All the time I was talking they went on looking at one another. It began to unnerve me.

When I stopped, Ernst said, 'This makes it worse.'

Millie nodded, putting the tip of a finger in her mouth and biting it viciously. 'I'm a fool,' she said.

'That is true,' said Ernst.

'But I meant to help,' she added defensively.

'So it was you who took the picture?' I said to her.

She nodded and bit harder than ever into her top knuckle, as if in self-chastisement.

'Some visky I think would be a good idea,' said Ernst gravely, and went to one of the old oak cupboards in the room, taking out a decanter and some handsome Bristol glasses. 'She meant to help,' he went on. 'She went over this morning to see you...' He paused suddenly. Again he and Millie exchanged one of their long stares, and as if strengthened by this, he asked abruptly, 'Vy did you come this evening, Marabelle?'

'Because I thought you had the picture,' I said.

'But Vy?'

'Because of the rose-petals on the floor in the study.'

He gave a nod of understanding, and handed me a glass of whisky. He swallowed his own whisky in one gulp, as if it were schnapps, and then sat waiting for it to take effect on him. 'Then the police too know that Millie took the picture?' he said.

'No, they think I took it,' I said. 'I was wearing one of your roses too.'

'Ah yes, of course. I picked three this morning, one for you, one for Beryl because I just saw her setting out with her bicycle, and one for Millie.'

'None for yourself?' I asked.

He shook his head. 'Flowers are for vimmen.'

'It was I who took the picture,' Millie said quickly.

'Ernie had nothing to do with it. And it was fearfully nice of you, Marabelle, not to tell the police anything about us. Ernie hates the police, you know.'

I wondered if she had said it too quickly. I felt that perhaps she had, yet I was not sure. I still kept thinking every now and then about Sholto's theory of someone from outside hiding in the cloakroom, and I was trying to remember whether or not I had ever seen Ernst

179

wearing one of his own roses. I had to admit that I could not remember having done so.

'I don't hate the police,' said Ernst. 'Here in Leckham I have had very good relations with them. But I think that as a foreigner I should be as inconspicuous as possible. It would be more comfortable perhaps if my name would be Vinnicott.'

'Anyway, Ernie had nothing to do with it,' Millie said again. 'What happened was this. I went over to Norman's this morning to see if you were still there and ask if you'd like to go to a sale with me this afternoon . . . I've missed the sale, of course, and there was a tallboy advertised that sounded exactly the thing I've been looking for for ages. Still, as I was saying, I went over, and I was passing Norman's study and happened to look inside and there was the Clegg. I recognised it, of course, because I've often heard Norman describe it. And the room was empty—that's to say, Basil was in it, but he went out just as I looked in. Well, I suppose if I'd stopped to think, I shouldn't have interfered, but I thought of that talk you had with Susan yesterday on the telephone, and the things you told me afterwards, and I thought if I just nipped in through the window and took the thing it might save you a lot of trouble. So that's what I did. And I meant to come over again and find you and tell you what I'd done, and then I suddenly remembered that the fishmonger sometimes has rabbits on a

Tuesday, so I dashed off, and when I got back the whole place was crawling with police. Of course I thought it was because of my having stolen the picture, and I was absolutely terrified. I've been sitting here trembling the whole day, wishing you'd come over so that I could explain things.'

'She's so stupid, so stupid, this voman!' Ernst cried passionately. 'When I got home this evening, she was sitting here afraid to turn on the lights because the police might come looking for her and say she was a thief. I said to her, "Ven you saw the police, you should have taken it back at *vunce*!"'

'But you know you hate having anything to do with the police!' Millie wailed. She turned to me. 'He got furious with me when I was had up once for riding without a rear-light. He was much more severe with me than the constable, who only said I might get into trouble if I did it again. It's because of the uniforms, you know. Ernie hates any one in uniform, after what he went through at home.'

'Anyway,' I said, feeling soothed by this story, which all seemed to me natural and in character and undoubtedly true, 'no harm's been done, since we've got the picture. I think the best thing will be for the the three of us to take it over together and tell the inspector what happened.'

They greeted this with silence.

'He seems to be quite a nice man,' I said to

181

encourage them.

'We can't,' said Ernst. 'We haven't got the picture.'

'Someone came and stole it,' said Millie, her voice shooting up into cockney shrillness. 'While I was sitting in the kitchen in the dark, hoping every one would think I was out and not come and question me, someone got into this room and stole the picture!'

'That,' said Ernst, 'is the frightful thing that has happened that I spoke of ven you came.'

CHAPTER SIXTEEN

That moment cured me for ever, I believe, of wanting to possess anything even moderately valuable. If the Roger Clegg had been simply a photograph of my grandmother and her three friends, picnicking in a meadow, none of this would have happened. The photograph would have been bundled into limbo long ago. There would have been no murder.

After a moment's thought, I said, 'Sholto took it.'

'You don't think it was Susan?' Ernst asked.

'I think it was Sholto—mostly because he's really the bit of the whole thing that I can't understand,' I said. 'Anyway, I shall go and accuse him of it and see what he says.'

'But why should Sholto come prowling

round here?' asked Millie. 'Did he know I'd taken the picture?'

'He probably knew about the rose-petals mixed up with the papers,' I said, 'and drew his own deductions. He knows that any roses about the place come from here. Besides, he may even have seen you. I'm not sure where he was at the time that Norman and Susan and I dashed into the hall. He didn't turn up there until some minutes later. He says he was in the garden, so he may have seen you running off with the picture under your arm.'

'I think it was Susan,' said Millie.

'No, Susan would have made a fuss if she'd found it here,' I said. 'She'd never have sneaked off with it without asking you what the hell you thought you were doing with it. After all, she'd have had a right to. It's her picture.'

'But vot does Sholto want it for?' asked Ernst.

'I wish I knew.'

In fact, my mind was becoming more and more of a muddle of contrary suspicions. Perhaps Sholto had taken the picture. Perhaps Sholto had committed the murder. Perhaps he had done one of these things, but not the other. Perhaps he had done neither. Perhaps he had not seen Millie running off with the picture. Perhaps he had done some thinking about the hypothetical man who had been hiding in the cloakroom, then some thinking about the rose-petals in the study, and then had come

183

prowling round the Weinkrauts' bungalow with some very unpleasant suspicions in his mind. I thought I would not say anything about this last possibility to Ernst or Millie.

'Well, I'm terribly sorry about it all,' said Millie. 'I only wanted to help. D'you think I ought to go to that policeman and tell him the whole thing?'

'In the morning,' I said. 'In the meantime I'll talk to Sholto and Susan and see if I can get anything out of either of them.'

I meant to do this as soon as I got back to the house. But when I did, I happened to hear a clock chiming, and realised that it was time for Norman's milk.

I found the bottle in the refrigerator. Tipping the milk into a saucepan, I heated it up, poured the milk into a jug and put the jug and a mug on a tray. Then I had one of my moments of housewifely competence. These always surprise me a little when they happen, and I tend to be rather impressed by them, and perhaps this is fortunate, for later I was quite certain of what I had done.

Remembering that milk bottles ought to be rinsed out and put on the doorstep for the milkman to collect the next morning, I assembled the day's empty bottles, rinsed them thoroughly at the tap and put them on the doorstep, feeling that pleasant glow of virtue that comes to me whenever I chance to do one of the things that I usually forget. At home

184

empty milk bottles usually increase in number until the milkman nearly batters the door down in his anxiety to get them back. And that was all I did just then in the kitchen. Absolutely all. I did not wash the saucepan in which I had heated the milk. I left it on the kitchen table, with the plates and glasses and other things left over from dinner.

Norman was in the study. He was alone and had apparently been trying to read, but when I walked in the book was lying face downwards on his knee and his hands were dangling over the arms of his chair.

'I'm sorry if I kept you waiting for this,' I said. 'I was over at the Weinkrauts' and didn't realise how late it was.'

He gave a smile. 'As a matter of fact, I'd forgotten all about it,' he said. 'I was sitting here, thinking. You're being very good to me.'

I put the tray down on the table beside him. 'D'you mind if I try telephoning a cable to John?' I asked. 'I'm not really sure where he is, but if I send it to the first place he stayed at, it might get sent on to him.'

'Go ahead,' said Norman, and picked up the jug of milk.

He sat there sipping the milk while I slowly dictated a cable to Holland. He had finished just about as I put down the telephone. He pushed the tray away.

'I suppose you'll be staying on now for a little while, won't you?' he said.

'I'll have to,' I said.

He looked as if he wanted to say something more, but he did not. I saw him run his tongue along his lips and grimace slightly, as if milk was not really his favourite drink, but as he went on saying nothing, I got up to go.

'Hadn't you better go to bed?' I said. 'You look awfully tired.'

'I'll go soon,' he said. 'I shouldn't sleep if I went now, and there's a letter I want to write. Marabelle—'

'Yes?'

'D'you know, I'm glad that Piers is dead—glad. I'm finding out some shocking things about myself to-day. But you might tell me something...'

I waited.

'D'you think Susan could have done it?'

As I did not answer, he smiled at me and said, 'All right, I know I shouldn't have asked that. But she's big enough, you know, and strong enough, and if she'd suspected what I told her this morning about Piers, she might have been angry enough. I'm feeling rather inclined to put my money on Susan. Good night.'

I said good night and went upstairs.

From the light showing under the door, I guessed that Sholto was in his room, but when I tapped on the door, it was Susan's voice that said, 'Come in.' She was lying on the bed, fully dressed, with her hands folded under her head and a cigarette between her lips.

I asked, 'Where's Sholto?'

'In the attic,' she said. 'I wasn't going to sleep another night in that frightful camp-bed, so I got Beryl to take his things up there. Where've you been all the evening?'

I told her, and after a moment's hesitation, told her about Millie having taken the picture and its third disappearance.

Like me, Susan said at once, 'Sholto's got it.' But she did not look much interested.

I leant on the edge of the bedstead. 'Look,' I said, 'about Sholto—'

She stopped me with a movement of her hand. 'Don't talk about him. D'you know, Norman actually wants me to marry Sholto again? Did you ever hear anything so crazy?'

'Well, he's used to Sholto,' I said.

'As if I should ever dream of marrying again!' she said. 'Besides, who'd want me. I'm too old and ugly. No, I shall have to consider the whole problem of my life in some completely new way. For instance, I might open a shop—hats or antiques or something. Or politics. But the one thing I definitely won't do is marry again—anyway, not Sholto. He's mean. That's what I never could stand about him. It isn't that he wants things for himself, but he wants to stop other people having them. That's why he came here. He doesn't care about the Roger Clegg, and he doesn't want the money he might get by selling it on the

187

quiet. He just wants to stop me having it, because he knows I'm fond of it. Then sooner or later he'll make a terrific thing out of giving it back to me, to show how much he loves me and how cruel I am to him, or something like that. Whatever one does, that's what it always comes back to.'

It struck me that amongst Sholto's failings, she had not included the probability that he had killed the husband who had succeeded him. I wondered whom she did suspect, and I was just thinking of asking her when she said, 'Now do get out, and leave me in peace. I'm completely exhausted. And you might see if you have any good ideas about things like hat shops. After all, you'd quite a long time on your own before you married John. You must have some notion of how one fills the time. Only don't tell me to write a play or a novel or anything, because I'm not clever like you. I really might try politics, only I'm not sure what party I belong to, and nowadays it's more important to decide about that than it used to be. Of course, I'm a Liberal at heart, but—'

I said good night and slipped out of the room before Susan could really settle down to the job of threshing out her political convictions on me.

But outside I came to a standstill, thought for a moment, then popped my head into her room again.

'By the way, you used to call Sholto

"Pussy," didn't you?' I said. 'What was it short for?'

'Oedipussy, of course. Him and his mother, you know.'

'Thanks.' I shut the door again and went up to the attics.

There were three of them, all with low, sloping ceilings and small Gothic windows at unexpected points. There was nothing in them but lumber, except for the two camp beds that had been placed side by side in the middle of the largest attic. Around the beds, on all sides, rose tiers of trunks, packing-cases and untidy heaps of dusty books. Near the window there were some odd lengths of linoleum, rolled up and tied with string and looking like organ-pipes jutting up into the cobwebby shadows, and here and there were piles of empty cardboard dress-boxes, saved against some unlikely day when a member of the family might want to indulge in an orgy of Christmas-present distribution. In the middle of it all I found Sholto sitting on one of the beds, smoking and reading one of the dusty books.

When he saw me, he smiled brightly and said, 'I rather thought you'd be along. Quite the busy little fairy around the place, aren't you? What can I do for you now?'

'What have you ever done for me?' I decided to lie down on the spare camp-bed, because suddenly I was so tired that it seemed to me impossible to go on standing upright for one moment longer. 'What have you done with that picture, Sholto?'

He turned a page in his book and asked absently, 'What picture?'

'You popped over to the Weinkrauts' when you thought no one was looking and took it,' I said. I added ingeniously, 'But Millie saw you.'

'Did she now?' he said, smiling again. 'Clever of her.'

'Come on,' I said, 'where have you put it?'

'Where d'you think?'

'Oh, do be reasonable,' I begged him. 'It's somewhere here. We could easily find it if we started looking for it.'

'Go ahead and look,' he said.

I had realised, of course, that searching for the picture in those attics would be a nightmare. The thing might be anywhere. Sholto knew that I had realised this, and was enjoying the fact. He also knew, I imagine, that I had not the slightest intention of doing any searching that night.

Stretching myself out on the camp-bed, I kicked my shoes off. 'Anyway, what d'you want with the damn' thing?' I asked. 'And what made you come here in the first place?'

'I told you, Susan bullied me into coming,' he said.

'She didn't. She was horribly upset at finding you here.'

He shook his head. 'She put that on just in case you took offence at her being afraid that you might not be adequate for the job.'

'No,' I said, 'you came here for some reason of your own.'

'Doesn't some sort of a selfish motive govern most human actions?'

'All right, all right,' I said. 'And now what?'

'Well then, I'll tell you.' He looked round for an ash-tray, failed to find one, took a match-box out of his pocket and carefully knocked his ash into that. Sholto had a streak of fanatical tidiness which did not allow him to drop the ash on the floor even in that unswept attic. 'Susan was perfectly right, as she so often is. I did come here to annoy her. I came here to find the picture and take it away with me, and keep it until I thought of something that I wanted to make her do—something that she'd really hate doing. Then I'd have promised her the picture in exchange for this, whatever it was.'

'I never knew you were such a horrid person,' I said.

'I'm not really horrid,' he said. 'I just had the feeling it would do me good to get my own back on Susan for once. I dare say it would have led to far better relations between us.'

'I suppose you know that Norman wants you and Susan to get married again,' I said.

He chuckled. 'Yes, we've been talking about it this evening. I'm all for it.'

I jerked up on an elbow. 'You *want* to marry Susan again?'

'Oh no, I don't mean that,' he said. 'But I'm

191

all for Norman's scheme. He's going to make a new will, and there's going to be a lot of money for Susan and me in it if we're married at the time of Norman's death, but otherwise it all goes direct to Maurice and Beryl.'

'With nothing for Susan?'

'Nothing for Susan.'

I looked carefully into his long, horse's face to see if he was serious. After a moment, against my own belief in Norman's judgment and good sense, I came to the conclusion that Sholto was both serious and delighted.

'And the idea is, I suppose, that you'll say no,' I said.

He nodded happily.

'You really are horrid,' I said. 'But you won't have the chance. Susan won't ask you. She's going to marry the detective-inspector. Besides, she'd like the children to have Norman's money.'

'You may be right,' said Sholto good-humouredly. 'I dare say you are. But still, if I go ahead and marry someone else as soon as Norman's changed his will, it'll show Susan what I think of her.'

'Seems a queer reason for taking such a drastic step,' I said.

'Oh, but I'm in love too.'

'Have you decided with whom?'

'Yes, with that beautiful girl I met last week. I've been thinking about her a lot since I got here, and now this idea of Norman's has just

192

given me the necessary push to do something about her. Unless, of course...' he stopped and started looking at me very oddly.

I had been taking unobtrusive glances around the attic, wondering where a search for the Clegg might profitably start, but that long, surprised stare from Sholto made me concentrate my attention on him again. 'Unless what?'

'I just had an idea,' he said. 'I was thinking about you and John. I was wondering if there was any chance of a reconciliation between you, because if not, I could easily fall in love with you. After all, you're the only woman I know who understands me.'

'I remember you once said that to me when you were very drunk,' I said. 'I've always felt since that it's come between us.'

'But d'you think that you and John will come together again?'

'In any case,' I said with a sigh, 'I shall never marry again.'

A slightly melancholy silence followed this remark, and I got up to go.

My huge bedroom felt chilly and ghostly when I got down to it and I hated the idea of going to bed. But I made myself undress quickly, before I could settle down to dreaming by the electric fire, got into bed and switched off the light. I thought I was so tired that I was sure to fall asleep immediately.

Instead, my tiredness seemed instantly to

drop from me and to leave me full of an aching desire for activity. For about half an hour I fought this, trying to control my feverish fidgets, which soon made me wreck the whole structure of my bedclothes. But then I got up, put on my dressing-gown and went downstairs. It had occurred to me that I could do the washing-up which I had intended to leave for Basil, and that the effort of doing this at one in the morning would certainly put me to sleep.

But the sight of the kitchen depressed me unbearably, and I wondered, not for the first time in my life, how I had ever managed to let myself slip into a position of domestic responsibility. The trouble is, I like cooking. I even like shopping. If I am deprived of either of these two activities for too long I become nervous and envious of any woman who is doing the job. But I hate cleaning anything, anything at all.

Luckily, as I stood there, feeling that to lift one finger to bring order to the kitchen would be torture, my eyes fell on the pots of paint that Basil had brought me. Here was the solution. I set to work, spreading newspapers on the floor, opening tins, finding an overall and some paint rags, and in about twenty minutes I was comfortably established in the hall, painting the door of the drawing-room. I knew from experience that it took me about an hour to put a coat of paint on a door and door frame and there were seven doors opening on to the hall.

Seven hours, I thought, would be too long a stretch, but at least in two or three hours I could make an impression on the place, so that Norman would have to go on and have something done about the rest of it. Basil had chosen a very pretty shade of duck-egg blue, and I was sure that in the long run, Norman would be grateful.

Actually far more painting was done that night than I had calculated when I started, for when I had been at it only half an hour, Beryl appeared, saying that she could not sleep and had come to find out what the queer smell was that had seeped up to her room. We managed to find an old brush in a cupboard, and she joined me in the painting.

We went on working till about four o'clock. By then I had stopped caring whether I slept for the rest of the night or not, and thought that a pot of tea and a book would help me comfortably through the remaining hours. I went into the kitchen and made the tea, while Beryl started tidying up the paint pots and newspapers.

We were just starting up the stairs together when Beryl thought of turning out the lights and put out a hand to the light switch.

I tried to stop her. 'Better leave it on, in case any one comes prowling around in the night,' I said. 'They might get against the wet paint and spoil it all.'

But I said it just too late. Before I had

195

finished speaking, Beryl had switched on the light of the landing above and switched off the light in the hall. That was how we came to notice the line of light showing under the door of Norman's study. If the light in the hall had been left burning we should never have seen it, but with the hall in darkness, the streak of light under the door of the study showed up brilliantly.

Beryl said, 'Look, he's left the light on.'

'Yes,' I said, 'he's left the light on.' I remember the sound of my own words, the note of false conviction in them, the eagerness to say just the same as Beryl in order to dodge away from my own sharp feeling that something was wrong. After all, every one leaves lights on now and then.

I pushed the tray into Beryl's hands and went quickly across the hall. I hoped that the door would be locked, because that would mean that everything was normal. But the door was not locked. I opened it and saw Norman sitting in the chair where I had left him. For an instant I thought he was asleep, but then I saw that I was badly mistaken.

CHAPTER SEVENTEEN

The most difficult thing to explain to the inspector, when he arrived, was my painting.

196

He thought, for some reason that I could not follow, that I had been trying to cover up finger-prints. I told him I thought he had already found as many finger-prints as he wanted in relation to the murder of Piers, while in relation to that of Norman, the only significant prints were my own on the door-handle of the study, and naturally I had not put any paint on the door handle.

Perhaps the inspector might not have been so difficult if he and some of his satellites had not got their coats against the wet paint, though in the course of their duties they must often have got their coats against worse things than a little paint of duck-egg blue. I told him that the smears would come off quite easily if he would let me get to work on them straight away with some turpentine. But he seemed to take this as another attempt on my part to destroy evidence.

The truth was I was more than a little lightheaded and was wishing that he would allow me to do something, instead of sitting still. For it was I who had killed Norman. It looked as if there could be no doubt of that. I had heated up the poisoned milk, carried it in to him and watched him drink it. I had even noticed the grimace he had made at the taste. Probably, I thought, he had believed that I had tried to give the milk some original flavour, and he had been too polite to protest. Politeness, it would seem, can be a dangerous virtue.

The inspector collected every one in the drawing-room. Susan and Beryl sat side by side, holding one another's hands, and Sholto sat uncomfortably on a small, upright chair in the corner of the room, looking as if he were trying to shrink away out of sight. He looked exceedingly guilty, but no one took any notice of it. The house was full of noise, of men tramping about and orders being given, and yet at the same time it seemed full of an oppressive silence.

There was a long pause while we waited for Mrs Fawcett. At last the constable who had been sent for her came down and said that her door was locked and that he could get no answer from her. The inspector told him to get the door open somehow and make her come down. As the constable went off again, the inspector started his questioning. He told us that what he wanted to establish at this point was the normal procedure with Norman's milk, from the time it was delivered at the house to the time he drank it, and also all that had happened to the particular pint of milk that had poisoned Norman. It seemed probable, the inspector told us, that the cause of death had been a heavy overdose of Norman's usual sleeping-tablets, dissolved in the milk, though this could not be certain until a post-mortem had been held. It was not impossible that Norman had taken the tablets

198

deliberately, but this did not seem likely, since shortly before his death he had written a letter to his lawyers asking for an appointment in a few days' time. By the time that all this had been explained, the constable had appeared once more.

'This did it,' he sad, holding up a key. 'Came from the door of the young lady's bedroom. Seems it fits most of the locks. But she isn't there.'

'The young lady?'

'No, the old one. This Mrs Fawcett.'

'Well, where is she?'

'Gone, I reckon, sir.'

'Gone,' said the inspector. 'Not in the house?'

The constable shook his head.

The inspector turned to Susan. 'What do you know about this, Mrs Beltane?'

Susan had a pale, shaky look, and her eyes looked a little mad. She was wearing a blue velvet housecoat, her face was greasy with cold cream and her hair uncombed. But her voice sounded normal. 'I know nothing about it, Inspector. I thought she was in bed. She took to her bed this morning as soon as these troubles began. I believe you saw her there.'

The inspector nodded. 'Who saw her last?'

'I saw her when I took her supper up to her,' said Beryl.

'Any one seen her since then?'

There was silence.

The inspector looked at the constable. 'What's the condition of her room?'

'Neat and tidy, sir,' said the constable. 'Bed's been made.'

'Personal belongings removed?'

'Not so far as I could tell, sir. Clothes are in the drawers, slippers by the bed. But there's no handbag or money in the room.'

Something made me interrupt. 'Are there a lot of silver things on the dressing-table?'

'Silver?' said the constable. 'No, miss.'

'No silver-backed brushes, and bottles with silver stoppers and so on?'

'No, miss.'

The inspector told me to explain why I had asked this question.

I said. 'This morning, before you came, I was sitting up there with Mrs Fawcett. She said she was frightened at being left alone. And I noticed an unusually fine set of silver on the dressing-table. I was just thinking that if she'd flitted suddenly, she might not have liked to leave it behind.'

The inspector took a long look at me, then said to Beryl, 'Miss Rice, did you notice this silver when you took the supper up?'

I did not like the implication of this question. It seemed to me that the inspector had immediately suspected that I had invented the silver in order to convince him of something or other concerning Mrs Fawcett.

But Beryl said, 'Yes.'

'Mrs Baynes,' said the inspector, 'at what hour of the night did you start on your painting operations?'

'About one o'clock,' I said.

'And from that time until I arrived you were either in the hall or had it in full view?'

I nodded.

'So that if Mrs Fawcett left this house, it must have been between the time Miss Rice took up her supper and the time you started painting. At what time did you go upstairs, Miss Rice?'

Beryl, Susan and I had a discussion on this point and agreed that it had been about eight o'clock.

'Now, Mrs Baynes,' said the inspector, 'you left the House about nine o'clock last night and paid a visit to your neighbours, Mr and Mrs Weinkraut.'

'Yes,' I said. 'How did you know that?'

'The house was under observation. But the man on duty followed you to see where you were going, and it might have been possible for Mrs Fawcett to slip out of the house unobserved at that time.'

'Are you suggesting,' I said, 'that I lured the man out of the way so that Mrs Fawcett could escape? If you want to know, I wouldn't have done such a thing, even if she'd asked me, because I didn't trust the woman.'

'I'm not suggesting anything,' he said. 'One other person left this house, but that was

201

before dinner.' He looked at Sholto.

Sholto gave a jerk in his chair, swallowed and said, 'Yes—yes, I know. I had to get out for a little. The house was beginning to do things to me.'

'You also went to see Mr and Mrs Weinkraut.'

'Yes, but no one was in.'

'Yet you went into the house.'

Sholto gave a nervous titter. 'I did, as a matter of fact. But I'd no idea I was being watched.'

'You came out, carrying a picture.'

'Yes, I did, didn't I?' said Sholto, and gave a loud crack to his knuckles.

Susan drew her breath in sharply.

'Was that the missing Roger Clegg?' asked the inspector.

'Yes,' said Sholto. 'I'd deduced the Weinkrauts had it.'

'A pity you kept you deductions to yourself. Where is this picture now?'

'I don't know,' said Sholto.

'You don't know?'

'No, I bought It back with me and hid it under my bed. That's the bed I slept in last night. But when I went up to the room later I found that all my things had been shifted out of it and that Mrs Beltane had moved in. And the picture was gone again.'

'Inspector,' cried Susan in a voice that was suddenly shrill with desperation, 'what has all this got to do with the death of Mr Rice? I don't care what's happened to that picture. I hate it. I never want to see it again. Let's get back to the milk.'

'In a moment,' said the inspector. 'Mr Dapple, You slept to-night in the attic, I believe. Had your things been taken straight up there?'

'Yes,' said Sholto, 'but not the picture.'

'And the last time you saw the picture was when you put it under Mrs Beltane's bed, shortly before dinner?'

'It was my bed,' said Sholto. 'It was my bed when I put the picture under it.'

'Don't believe him, Inspector,' said Susan. 'He's one of the worst liars I know. Why, he's as good as admitted that he meant to steal the picture.'

'I hadn't actually decided what to do with it,' said Sholto gloomily. 'And it doesn't matter now, since it's gone again.'

'He's hidden it somewhere,' said Susan. 'But I don't care. He can have it. Any one can have it. I don't want it any more. I hate it.'

'Miss Rice, did you see this picture under the bed when you moved Mr Dapple's things upstairs,' the inspector asked.

'No,' said Beryl.

'To return to the milk then. Who first handled the bottle when it was delivered to the house?'

'I did,' I said. Then I caught myself up. 'No, I

203

didn't, it was Basil. He found the bottles on the doorstep when he arrived and brought them in with him.'

'And you took them from him?'

'Yes, and put them in the refrigerator.'

'And when did you handle them next?'

'I didn't handle the T.T. bottle until late yesterday evening, when I took it out and heated up the milk in it for Mr Rice, as I've told you. The others I handled earlier, when I was cooking.'

Susan put in, 'I handled the T.T. bottle at dinner. Mrs Fawcett had told my sister that she didn't want anything to eat but would like some hot milk, so I heated it up for her and my daughter took it upstairs. But I made the mistake of taking out the T.T. bottle, and I was just going to open it when my sister told me to put it back and take one of the other bottles.'

'You didn't actually open the bottle?' asked the inspector.

'No,' said Susan. 'That is...' Her eyes grew suddenly intent. 'No, I didn't open it, but I did jab my nail through the top.'

'Please tell me exactly what happened.'

'Well, you see, I just grabbed the first bottle that came to hand,' said Susan, 'and that was the T.T. bottle. And as I was doing it, I automatically jabbed my nail through the metal top, because that's the way I always take tops off milk bottles. And at that point I was told I'd taken the wrong bottle, so I put it back in the refrigerator and took another. That's all.'

'So that from that time the top of the T.T. bottle had a tear in it?'

'Yes.'

'A large tear?'

'Fairly. It must have been split right across.'

'Mrs Baynes,' said the inspector, 'when you heated the milk up in the evening, did you notice this tear?'

'Of course,' I said.

He looked thoughtfully from one to the other of us as if he were trying to work something out, then he spoke again to Susan. 'Mrs Beltane, when you handled the T.T. bottle, was the top intact?'

'Yes, I think so,' she said. 'I...' She stopped. She frowned. With one hand she began to smooth the velvet over her knees. 'D'you know, I'm really not sure about that. I wasn't looking at it, I just jabbed at it with my thumb nail, as I told you. But now you ask me...'

He waited patiently.

She made a gesture of helplessness. 'Honestly, I can't say for sure. But if there was a puncture it must have been a very small one.'

The inspector said nothing, still looking at Susan reflectively. I began to think that perhaps I had been wrong about him, because I did not think that many men had looked at Susan with just that expression on their faces.

There was a good deal more of it. He went

over and over the same ground, putting his questions about the handling of the milk bottle in a slightly different form each time, trying to see if he could lead up to that last question he had asked Susan in such a way as to startle her uncertain memory into life. But Susan went on saying that although there might have been a puncture in the metal, she could not swear to it, one way or the other.

After a time I said, 'Won't the milk bottle top itself tell you anything? You'll probably find it in the sink basket in the scullery. I think that's where I put it.'

'We have the top already,' he answered, 'and it's split in two. And the milk bottle itself has been thoroughly rinsed and put out on the doorstep. And the saucepan in which the milk was heated has been carefully washed. You did the murderer's work for him most efficiently, Mrs Baynes. I congratulate you.'

I nodded sympathetically. I could see that he was very tired and very irritable from interrupted sleep. I am sure that if he had been feeling better himself, he would never have said such a detestable thing.

Then I jumped. 'Wait!' I said. 'The saucepan?'

'Yes, everything else in the kitchen is in a mess, and just one saucepan washed and left to drain by the sink.'

'But that can't be the milk saucepan,' I said, 'because I didn't wash it. I left it on the table

206

with everything else.'

'There's no saucepan on the table, and there's no saucepan that has any remains of milk in it.'

'Well, I didn't wash it,' I said. 'What's more, I don't see how any one else can have done it, because I remember distinctly seeing it on the table when I came down to get the paint. And after that, no one but Beryl and I went into the kitchen until you got here, and I know Beryl didn't do any washing-up. After all, I was in the hall all the time and I'd have noticed any one who went to the kitchen.'

He gave me one of his puzzling stares, and I knew that he did not believe me.

He let us go soon after that, and by force of habit, because it was the place where I expected to be left alone, I wandered out to the kitchen.

It was early morning by then, and a little weak light was beginning to show in the sky. The kitchen looked unbearably squalid. Leaving the washing-up for Basil to do in the morning had turned out to be a very bad idea. Looking round I was filled with an enormous disgust.

Yet in some way, the mess made it easier not to think of Norman. I was feeling sick, and I made myself believe that this had something to do with revulsion at the litter of unwashed plates and knives and forks and cooking-pots. But the milk saucepan had been washed and was upside down on the draining board.

Sitting down in the middle of it all I lit a cigarette and then began to cry. I longed for John and for my own home, and for the time to be a year hence, or else a week ago.

After a while, with the tears still dripping, I began to tidy up the kitchen. But I had scarcely piled three plates together when a policeman appeared in the doorway.

'None of that,' he said sternly, and looked at me as if I had walked right into some trap that he had laid for me.

'Why not?' I asked furiously. 'It's too late to go to bed and I'd sooner have something to do.'

'That's right,' he said. 'Very sensible too. But no destroying evidence.'

'Is this evidence?' I asked, gesturing at the table.

'Who can tell?' he replied. 'The saucepan's evidence.'

'That's right, now you mention it,' I said.

'You just leave everything the way it is till the inspector tells you otherwise,' he said. 'If you want a change, why not take a stroll round the garden?'

'The idea doesn't tempt me,' I said. 'But if I could make some coffee, I'd take it to bed with me.'

He looked round cautiously, considering giving me permission to do this. His gaze slid over shelves and cupboards, seeking for utensils he could allow me to use because they could not by any stretch of the imagination be thought to have any connection with the poisoning. I stood watching him, following his gaze.

Suddenly I gave an exclamation. The constable had just taken a look at the mantelpiece, and I was hoping that he would not instruct me to make coffee in the blue and white ginger-jar that held a bunch of tapers, or a dusty-looking present from Margate, when I realised that Mrs Fawcett's gallery of past employers was missing.

'All the dead gentlemen!' I cried.

'What?' said the constable.

'All Mrs Fawcett's dead men,' I said. 'She had a row of them there. They've gone.'

'Now then,' said the constable, stern again. 'There never was no dead man in this kitchen. You take hold of yourself, my dear. You just sit down for a minute and calm yourself. And no tricks,' he added as an after-thought. 'I've been warned about you.'

'Tricks?' I said, staring at the empty space on the mantelpiece and trying to think.

'Like paint.'

'Listen,' I said, 'Mrs Fawcett, the housekeeper, whom you know perfectly well has disappeared, and who is unquestionably a very suspicious character, used to keep a row of photographs on that mantelpiece. The photographs were of her former employers, and the most important thing about them was that they were all elderly men, that they'd all died from stomach trouble, and they all left Mrs Fawcett what she called a little bit of money.' I turned my stare on him and hoped that it would penetrate him.

'Photographs?' he said slowly. 'A row of photographs, you say? Did any one else see them?'

'Of course,' I said. 'They weren't a vision of the departed vouchsafed to me alone. They were always up there on the mantelpiece. But they aren't there now. They're gone. She's taken them.'

He began to nod his head. He took it in very slowly, and was even slower making up his mind what to do about it. Before he had decided, there was a rush of footsteps in the passage and Beryl came running into the kitchen. Her face was blotched with crying, her hair was dishevelled and she had a good many paint smears on her dressing-gown, showing that she had taken no care of what she had touched. She stopped dead as soon as she saw the constable.

'What is it?' I asked.

She hesitated, looking at me intently and breathing fast, then she spoke in a low voice. 'My photograph of Daddy,' she said, 'the big one I had on my dressing-table...'

'Gone,' I said.

CHAPTER EIGHTEEN

Together we went to talk to the inspector. We told him about the disappearance of Norman's photograph and of the photographs from the kitchen. Some cursory searching was done. Nothing was found.

'Looks as if she took them with her, along with her silver toilet-set,' said the inspector. 'Seems they must have been her most valued possessions.'

'But my photograph of Daddy wasn't here,' said Beryl tearfully, 'and it's the only one I have.'

Susan put an arm round her. 'We can get another made,' she said.

'But why did she want it?' asked Beryl.

I said, 'I think I can tell you that.'

They all looked at me. Feeling nervous, because I knew that what I was going to say was not the kind of thing that should ever be said lightly, I said, 'Mrs Fawcett was a poisoner.'

'Eh?' said the inspector.

'Yes, she was one of those women—you've heard of them'—I said, 'who go from one domestic situation to another, polishing off their employers. And I believe those women are sometimes quite attached to their victims, and look after them very tenderly, and

211

sometimes they kill for profit, but sometimes for no particular reason, I suppose rather like a prostitute who sometimes sleeps with a man without being paid for it, just for the joy of it, so to speak.'

The inspector looked interested and said, 'Tell me more.'

I did not like his tone. 'As a matter of fact,' I said, 'I've known this almost since I got here. It's been worrying me terribly.'

'Then why didn't you happen to mention it to any one?'

'Because it was only an intuition—one that I couldn't quite understand and didn't really believe in. And I did do something about it. I told Norman he ought to let Mrs Fawcett know in some casual way that he wasn't leaving her anything in his will.'

'And what did he say to that,' asked the inspector.

'He said he couldn't possibly do it because it would have been an insult.'

'And you said?'

'What could I say?'

'What indeed?' The inspector was looking at me in the unfriendliest way possible. 'Mrs Baynes, if your very interesting theory is correct—'

I interrupted him. 'I know you're laughing at me, but you just wait and see. You'll find there was something very odd indeed about Mrs Fawcett.'

'I was going to say,' he said, 'that if your theory is correct, we must postulate either that the murder of Piers Beltane had nothing to do with that of Mr Rice, or else that a very small and elderly woman was capable of murdering a man by hitting him on the head with a hammer.'

I had a feeling that a detective-inspector should not use a word like postulate; it is the kind of word which suggests that one may get into deep water at any moment.

'She might have had an accomplice,' I said.

'One of the family?'

'No, of course not.'

'An outsider?'

I remember Sholto's theory. I began to get excited. 'Yes, an outsider who was hiding in the cloakroom, hoping to get a word with Mrs Fawcett when Piers walked in and discovered him.'

'Why didn't he simply come to the back door?'

'Perhaps there were reasons why he couldn't. Perhaps...' Suddenly I saw light, and my excitement increased so much that I felt quite cold. 'Her husband,' I said, 'the husband she wouldn't talk about. She'd have talked about him if he was dead, like all her employers, but he was alive and in some way a shame to her. Perhaps he'd been in prison, or ... Inspector, has any one escaped from prison recently?'

'Dozens of 'em,' said the inspector. 'They're always doing it. They simply won't listen when we tell them it's wrong.'

'But this is serious,' I said, 'terribly serious. Please listen to me. If I'm wrong, what's happened to Mrs Fawcett? Why has she run away?'

'A great many people don't like our faces,' he replied, 'even if they aren't poisoners. That's one of the tragedies of being on the police force.'

'And why did she take Mr Rice's photograph, if she wasn't keeping a picture-gallery of her victims?'

'That's an important question, certainly.' He added soberly, 'And I agree with you to this extent, that I think there is something odd about Mrs Fawcett which requires investigating. But although motiveless murders do occur, I do, on the whole, prefer a motive. I prefer to investigate the people with a motive; for instance, the people who *have* been left money. Do you know that Mr Rice was about to alter his will? There was a letter about that, which he had just written to his lawyers lying on his desk.' He walked out of the room, and we heard him tramping upstairs with the two other men.

Susan, who still had her arm round Beryl, absently dabbing at her eyes from time to time, gave me a worried look. 'D'you really believe all that about Mrs Fawcett being a poisoner,

Marabelle?' she asked.

I nodded. 'I've been watching that woman ever since I got here. Before there was any question of death here, I'd noticed her morbid interest in death. I saw her bring the hot milk to Norman—'

'Yes, but wait a minute,' said Susan. 'D'you mean she's been poisoning him slowly—that it's been going on for some time?'

'Well, he'd been getting pains for some weeks,' I said, 'from what he said was an ulcer. But I think that when they do the post-mortem they won't find an ulcer at all. What they'll find is arsenic.'

'But it was his own sleeping-pills that killed him,' said Susan. 'Or so they think, from the symptoms.'

'Because something had gone wrong. The murder of Piers, in fact. Mrs Fawcett never meant that to happen, and it brought the police and danger on the scene. So she decided to finish things off quickly and make a getaway.'

'You're wrong,' said Susan, 'you're quite wrong. And I'll tell you why. Norman wasn't murdered at all. He committed suicide.'

That brought a sudden wail from Beryl. She sprang to her feet, looking round wildly at us all.

'That isn't true! I know what you mean, and it isn't true, any of it!' She was tense and trembling, and two spots of colour blazed feverishly in her cheeks. 'You're going to say he murdered Piers, because of me, and then killed himself! But it isn't true!' Again she started crying violently and rushed out of the room.

Susan got up to follow her. But in the doorway she paused. 'That is what I was going to say,' she said, 'and it's what the inspector thinks too.'

'Has he told you so?' I asked.

'No, but I can tell,' she said. 'It's easy to tell what a man like that is thinking.' She went out after Beryl.

For a moment I thought that I was alone in the room for Sholto had been so quiet that I had forgotten him. But as Susan went out, he got up, stretched, yawned, then crossed the room and helped himself to a drink.

'You're doing the murderer's work for him very efficiently, Marabelle,' he said. 'It's quite obvious to any one that Mrs Fawcett is simply a red herring in this story.' Gulping the drink, he helped himself to another, crossed to the sofa, sat down in the middle of it and stretched his legs out in front of him.

'It's now quite obvious,' he went on, 'why Piers was murdered. It was practically speaking an accident. That's to say, it was in the form of a most unwelcome necessity— unwelcome because it brought the police on the spot too soon and increased the risk of discovery. The real murder was the murder of Norman.'

He gulped the second drink, immediately

216

got up again and helped himself to a third. I hoped he was not going to get drunk. He got drunk very easily and always very suddenly.

'The murderer was someone who was not supposed to be in the house at all,' he said, returning to the sofa. 'We shall probably find that, whoever he was, he has an excellent alibi for the time when Piers was murdered. He was hiding in the cloakroom, waiting for an opportunity to slip into the kitchen and poison the milk, when Piers walked in and found him.'

'Why didn't Piers call out?' I asked. I was not much disposed to listen to his theory because I was fairly sure about my own, but I thought that, if I kept him talking, he might forget to go on drinking. Sholto drunk was always very aggressive, argumentative and hard to handle.

'Because he saw nothing wrong in the person being there,' said Sholto. 'He wouldn't be able to guess, at a glance, that he was destroying a carefully prepared alibi. So the person probably kept Piers talking for a moment, and even reached out and put on Norman's mackintosh; to prevent blood getting on to his own clothes—I think he must have done that— it's a point that's been worrying me, because the murderer must have known that he might be seen anywhere, out in the road or wherever he went, and I think that's what he must have done. The inspector says there was a great deal of blood on Norman's mackintosh. Anyway, let's suppose that was it. Well then, without warning he clamped his hand over Piers' mouth to prevent his yelling, and then smashed him on the head with the hammer.'

I got up and helped myself to a drink. 'And where did he go from there?'

'The kitchen, of course.'

'But wouldn't he have been afraid of being seen?'

'I think he was seen.'

I looked at him blankly for a moment, then I saw what he meant. 'By Mrs Fawcett!'

'Exactly.'

'But then why should she clear out? Why not stay and denounce him?'

'There are various possibilities,' said Sholto. 'First, it's just possible that she didn't understand what she saw. Consider it. She saw someone come out of the cloakroom, go to the kitchen, take a bottle of milk out of the refrigerator, fiddle with it in some way and put it back, and then probably leave by the back door. Provided the person was someone she knew, whom it was not too surprising to see moving about familiarly in the house, why should she think that she had just seen a murderer?'

'But then why leave so suddenly?'

'She may have been intending to leave anyhow. In fact, d'you know what I've been wondering ever since I heard she'd gone? I've been wondering if we're going to find anything else missing besides Beryl's photograph of

Norman.'

I looked at him with respect.

'But we ought to go and tell the inspector this,' I said. 'He may not have thought of it.'

'Wait,' said Sholto. 'Let me finish what I was going to say. I'm sort of working it out as I go along, and it's a help having someone to listen. I said, that's the first possibility. But there are one or two others. One is that she saw the murderer and understood perfectly well what he was doing, and ran away because she knew he knew she had seen him, and was afraid of what he might do to her. That fits rather well with the way she behaved when Piers' body was found. She was altogether too upset for a woman who's apparently seen as much of death as she has, then she took to her bed and locked herself in. And the remaining possibility is that she'd decided on blackmail.'

'I suppose the police will find her quite easily,' I said.

Sholto was back at the whisky once more. 'Oh yes, they'll find her. But they may not find her in time.'

'In time for what?'

'To save her. Blackmail's a dangerous game when you're dealing with someone who's already committed two murders.'

'I still think she may have done the murders herself,' I said. 'You know, she fascinates me. I've just begun thinking I might write a play about her. And that would be my solution—I

219

should make her a murderess with a convict husband, of whom, in her respectability, she's deeply ashamed. Only I'm not quite sure why she never murdered him.'

'I don't think I'll tell you my solution,' said Sholto. He said it in a new tone of dramatic mystery. The whisky, I thought, was beginning to work. 'No, I'll keep my ideas to myself. How does it concern me, anyhow. I'm alive. Nobody's murdered me yet.' He looked at me challengingly, as if he thought I was going to contradict this. 'But I'm going carefully, let me tell you. I look behind doors when I go into a room. I'm taking no risks.'

'Aren't you afraid that that whisky might be poisoned?' I asked hopefully.

'No, because this murderer picks his victims carefully,' said Sholto, 'and any one might drink this. You're drinking it. No, as long as I do what other people do, I'm safe. But empty rooms are dangerous, and special dishes.' Then he calmed down suddenly and smiled. 'As a matter of fact, that was just talk. You know what I'm like. I dramatise things. But I don't actually think I'm in any danger, unless it turns out that I know something that I don't realise. That's always possible. And that makes it all the more important not to talk unnecessarily.'

'But why should any one want to murder Norman?' I said. 'What was he doing to any one?'

'He was doing something to me,' said
220

Sholto. 'He was trying to make me marry Susan.'

'And you were as pleased about that as could be. If Norman had really altered his will in the way he said he was going to, it would have given you the opportunity you were longing for, of spurning Susan publicly. But talking of the will, who was going to suffer by the new one?'

'Susan, of course,' said Sholto.

That was the thought that had been stirring uneasily in my mind all the time that I had been sitting there.

'I wonder when Norman told her about that idea of his,' I said. 'I wonder if it was before or after dinner.'

'What has that got to do with it?'

'Only that it was during dinner that she jabbed her nail through the cap of the bottle.'

'Preparing for the dirty work, so to speak? Ingenious but not really relevant, because you're forgetting something. The murder of Norman had already been decided on in the morning.'

'Because of Piers?'

He nodded.

'Then the new will can't have had anything to do with it.'

'Unless Norman had already had ideas in that direction, and had spoken of them to somebody. That trouble with Beryl and Piers had upset him profoundly, and he may have

221

been planning anything. But, as you say, it looks as if the new will had nothing to do with it. But there's always his old will. There may have been all sorts of people who were expecting money from him.'

'And one of them was hiding in the cloakroom when Piers walked into it?'

'Exactly.'

'Who?'

'Perhaps John,' he said casually.

'*John!*' I said.

'You told me a very phoney story about where he was when I arrived,' he said. 'I was fool enough to believe you at first and to sympathise with you. I thought you were frightfully brave. I thought, from the way you were taking it, you were just the sort of woman a man might safely think of marrying. But Susan told me it was all nonsense, and since then I've been wondering...'

To my own consternation, I found myself beginning to giggle. Which of us was drunk, I wondered, Sholto or me?

'You're just saying that to revenge yourself on me,' I said. 'John's in Holland.'

'How do you know?'

'Because that's where he told me he was going.'

'Do you get anything under Norman's will?'

'I don't know. Why should I? In any case, John's in Holland. If your theory's right and somebody was hiding in the cloakroom, it

222

wasn't John.'

'Well, who was it?'

I had no chance to answer him, because suddenly there was a commotion in the hall. I heard a man's voice angrily raised, and one or two others gruffly answering him. Then the door of the drawing-room opened and Maurice walked in, followed by two constables.

CHAPTER NINETEEN

Assured of who he was, the constables left him. From his face it was plain that Maurice had heard the news.

'You got here quickly,' I said.

'There's a train soon after five,' he said. 'Mother telephoned me. Where is she?'

'She went upstairs with Beryl.'

'Have they found out who did it?'

'Not yet.'

He gave me a haunted look and turned to go. He seemed far younger than when I had seen him last. He had stopped being a young man and become a burdened child. He wanted his mother for the comfort she could give him rather than the support he could give her, but he was holding himself in, trying to conceal his feelings.

'Just a moment, Maurice.' Sholto's voice

was startlingly loud and aggressive. The whisky was really at work now in its characteristic way. 'I'd like to talk to you.'

Maurice gave him a look. He knew Sholto well enough to recognise what had happened to him, and his lips closed into a hard line. In a few years Maurice's face was going to be stern and rather arrogant, unless something happened to humanise him.

'I'd like to ask you one or two questions,' said Sholto, 'just to clear up something in my own mind.'

Maurice still said nothing. But he still waited.

Sholto paused, then shot the question at him. 'What were you doing yesterday morning?'

'This and that,' said Maurice.

'Not good enough,' said Sholto. 'To begin with, where were you?'

Maurice's face grew whiter. 'Where I was supposed to be.'

'Where was that?'

'Why d'you want to know?'

'For your own good, my dear boy,' said Sholto, growing excited again. 'I want to help you. You may be in difficulties unless you've a sound explanation ready of where you were yesterday morning.'

'Why yesterday morning?' asked Maurice. His voice was soft and strangled. He was incredibly angry, but as always, trying to keep that fact to himself.

'Because that's when someone bashed Piers' head in, and put poison in your father's milk.'

Maurice did not answer.

Sholto went on, 'Someone came here to poison Norman, someone who knew that every day there was a special bottle of milk for Norman. That person hid in the cloakroom, waiting for a chance to get to the kitchen without being seen. Piers walked in unexpectedly, with the Roger Clegg, which he had hidden after Norman's visit to Susan, to make her think that Norman had stolen it, so that she would force her way in to find it in spite of Norman's objections to her coming here. Piers meant to plant the Clegg quietly in the cloakroom. But he saw someone in the cloakroom. Since he did not call out, it must have been someone he knew. But it was someone who did not want to be seen by any one, whose whole plan would be spoilt if Piers remarked on having seen him. And so this person took a hammer he saw on the shelf—' He stopped, looking surprised, for Maurice had just walked out of the room.

I shook my head wearily. 'Of all the preposterous things to do!'

He nodded earnestly.

'If I didn't know, from the way that I often behave myself,' he said, 'that extraordinary behaviour isn't necessarily suspicious behaviour, I should be inclined to say that that

225

was very suspicious.'

'I didn't mean that,' I said. 'I meant that you were practically accusing him of murdering his father, when the poor boy's hardly had time yet to get used to the idea that his father's dead.' I was really indignant.

'That's right,' said Sholto. 'I'm accusing everybody. First of all, I accused myself, but no one would listen to me. Now I'm accusing every one else in turn. I've accused Susan, and you and John, and Maurice. Beryl's next.'

'You're horribly drunk,' I said. 'If you say anything of the sort to that child, I will become a murderess.'

A silence followed. Sholto frowned and closed his eyes. I closed my eyes too. For a moment it felt wonderful. It seemed to me years since I had heard such a silence. I thought that I must have been sitting there for an eternity, listening to Sholto theorise, but that at last I had somehow managed to slip over the edge of existence into a void of darkness and quiet. It was very calming to my nerves, and I began to do a little thinking on my own, uninterrupted by Sholto.

I thought about Mrs Fawcett. I could see nothing seriously against my idea that she had poisoned Norman and that her convict husband had killed Piers. There was, of course, the point that Sholto had made concerning the fact that Piers had not raised any alarm on meeting his murderer in the cloakroom. But did that really supply grounds for Sholto's assumption that Piers must have known his murderer? Suppose, for instance, Piers had unexpectedly come on Basil in the cloakroom, would he have shouted? Even I had not shouted on that first morning, years and years ago, when Basil had walked into the kitchen and immediately locked himself into the scullery to change his trousers. Strange men walking about our homes raise very little comment provided they appear to know what they are doing, and if Piers had found a strange man attending to the taps, or doing something with a screwdriver to the pegs on the wall, he would probably only have said, 'Good morning,' and passed some democratic remarks on Arsenal, or whatever he thought would make a good impression.

But in that case, why had Mr Fawcett found it necessary to hit Piers on the head with a hammer? If Piers had seen nothing suspicious about him, why should Mr Fawcett have upset this satisfactory state of affairs by committing a murder? He must have known that in any case he was taking a risk, hiding in the cloakroom, and unless he had taken refuge there prepared to murder any one who came into it, in which case he might have had a pile of corpses on his hands before he managed to escape, it did perhaps seem a little unlikely that he should instantly have taken such drastic action. Perhaps there was something inadequate about my theory after all.

But I still liked it. I still felt that even if it was not much use as a solution to the problem of the two murders, it had dramatic possibilities, and that since nobody would let me go on painting the hall or washing-up the dishes, I might start plotting out a play instead. I opened my eyes, meaning to look around for some paper and a pencil, and saw that Sholto's long and unusual silence was accounted for by the fact that he was no longer in the room.

In a vaguely irritated way I thought, 'What's he up to now?' and then leant back and closed my eyes again. I thought that in all probability Sholto was somewhere upstairs, busily concealing the Roger Clegg. I was quite sure that he still had it, however hard he had tried to make it appear that Susan had hidden it. But I felt sure that if I went after him to see where he was putting the picture, the inspector would think that there was something suspicious about my actions and put a stop to them.

But no one, I thought, could stop me thinking out the plot of a play about Mrs and Mr Fawcett, which might some day actually make me a lot of money, always supposing that I could prevent it developing into something too Sunday-Societyish.

I decided that there would be just two characters in the play, the Fawcetts themselves. All the action would take place in the kitchen. By implication, a whole family would fill the rest of the house, but none of its members would appear. Perhaps the profile of the milkman might be glimpsed, passing the window, or perhaps one might just hear his whistling and the clink of the milk bottles on the doorstep ... I sat bolt upright with my eyes wide open, and Susan, coming in at that moment, said, 'Whatever are you staring at?'

She was very haggard, and had a more frightened look in her eyes than I had ever seen there.

'Nothing,' I said. 'But I'd just thought of something.'

'About these awful things?' She dropped on to the sofa and took her head in both hands. She had her handbag with her, and as she sat down it fell to the ground.

'It was nothing important,' I said. 'What's been happening?'

'Questions, questions, questions. And that creature Sholto dropping the most frightful insinuations about every one. And it was all his doing that the inspector got on to the fact almost immediately that Maurice hasn't got an alibi.'

'For yesterday morning?'

She looked up and nodded drearily. 'At least the silly boy won't say where he was. You know how difficult it is to make him say anything whatever at the best of times? Well, now he simply clamps his mouth shut and

229

won't say a word to anybody.'

'But Maurice adored Norman,' I said.

'Of course he did.'

'Then why's he doing it?'

'God knows. I'm too tired to think.' She stooped and picked up her bag. It came open as she did so and several things fell out of it, among them a cigarette-case. She swore mildly, picked up the case, opened it and offered a cigarette to me. I took one, and was reaching down to the carpet for her lighter when, amongst the other things there, I noticed a small photograph. It was of a face I knew, a man's. It was John's.

She saw me recognise it. Our eyes met. Then she stooped again, as if she were going to pick up the things that had fallen out of her bag, but as I spoke, she paused.

My voice came out so unevenly that it made me furious with myself. 'That's a ridiculously flattering photograph. He isn't nearly so good-looking really.' This was true. Yet I kept a print of the same photograph in a note-case in my own bag, because I liked it so much. That is to say, I had liked it up to that moment.

'Oh, don't you think so?' she said. 'I've always thought that John was very good-looking. But as a matter of fact I didn't mean you to see that, at any rate not until—' She stopped, for Sholto had just come in. Turning on him with a snarl, she cried, 'Can't you keep out of the way for ten minutes at a time? Have

230

you got to be under my feet wherever I go? I want to talk to Marabelle.'

'Sorry,' said Sholto, coming in and sitting down. 'The inspector sent me along. I think he wants to collect every one here again. He seems to have found out something of interest about Mrs Fawcett.'

Five minutes ago I should have felt excited. But now I had only one concern in my mind, which was to hide the terrible fear that had stabbed my heart. I was sure that my face was dead pale, and that every one who came into the room would be able to see how I was trembling, and the thought of that revolted my pride. However Susan had come by that photograph, and for whatever reason she carried it about with her in her handbag, she was not going to see what the sight of it in her possession had done to me.

Sholto was going on, 'About Maurice, Susan—'

'Be quiet!' she screamed at him. 'Don't say a word to me!'

'But I've got to,' said Sholto. 'Susan, if Maurice doesn't tell the truth about where he was yesterday morning—'

She put her hands over her ears.

Sholto turned to me with a shrug of his shoulders. Although his behaviour was quiet at the moment, he looked fairly drunk, which meant he was unpredictable. I thought of escaping to my own room. But then it occurred to me that perhaps I ought not to leave Susan and Sholto alone together, considering the mood that each was in, and while I hesitated, the inspector came in again. Maurice and Beryl followed him.

Susan stooped quickly to gather up John's photograph and the other things that had fallen out of her bag. She pushed them back into the bag in an untidy handful and snapped the bag shut. But she had not been in time. I had seen the inspector's gaze sharpen momentarily as he caught a glimpse of a man's picture.

Susan stood up and faced him, clutching the bag with both hands. She looked unnecessarily defiant, unless, of course, the defiance was really directed at me rather than at the inspector. If it was, I thought, she was going to need all that she had and more.

'Can't you do anything with your son, Mrs Beltane?' said the inspector. 'He still refuses to say a word about where he was yesterday morning. He knows nobody's accusing him of anything, but he keeps that mouth of his shut like a trap.'

Susan looked at Maurice, while Beryl quietly moved nearer to him. He took no notice of either of them. He was staring in a blind way at the spot on the carpet where John's photograph had lain.

'Maurice—' Susan began tentatively, then gave up and looked back at the inspector. 'No,

I don't think I can do anything with him,' she said softly. 'Nobody's ever been able to make Maurice say anything that he didn't want to. But anyway it isn't of any importance. Probably he was with a girl, and it embarrasses him to say so. He never says anything about that sort of thing to any one.'

She waited a moment hopefully, but there was no flicker of response on Maurice's face.

With her voice a little louder and firmer, she went on, 'But it isn't important. And I'll tell you why. It's because I'm the person who was waiting for Piers in the cloakroom. And I'm the person who put the poison in Norman's milk.'

There was silence. I saw Maurice shudder, and I saw also that the inspector was still watching Maurice, not Susan.

Then Sholto made a queer crowing sound, something between a cough and a hysterical laugh, and exclaimed, 'But in God's name, why?'

'Because I happen to be in love with another man,' said Susan, 'and Piers refused to release me. He said he'd never release me, and that if I simply left him, he'd follow me and make my life a hell. He'd have done it too. He had a very cruel streak in him.'

I could not interpret the expression on the inspector's face, but he did look at Susan now.

'But why did you have to murder your former husband as well, Mrs Beltane?' he asked. 'Would he also have followed you and made your life a hell?'

'Of course not,' she said. 'But he was going to alter his will. With Piers dead I had to have money, and under the new will I should have had nothing, unless I remarried Mr Dapple.'

'Then your new—' The inspector hesitated, then said deliberately, 'lover—has no money?'

'Not enough,' said Susan. 'Besides, I know he'd insist on treating his present wife generously when he left her.'

I started to get up. At last the frozen feeling had gone out of me, and I was hot with blazing anger.

But Sholto spoke before I could. 'I wonder why you think that Norman left you anything in his first will, Susan.'

CHAPTER TWENTY

Something happened to Maurice's face. It looked for a moment, from the grimace he made, as if he had just had a violent pain in his inside. Then something approaching a smile softened his grim mouth.

'He didn't,' he said.

We all looked at him, and he immediately showed signs of freezing up again.

Very encouragingly, the inspector said, 'Yes?'

Every one waited. It was as if a parrot,

234

guaranteed to have an interesting vocabulary, but which had been silent for ten years, had suddenly spoken one word and then snapped its beak shut again.

'What d'you mean, Maurice?' Susan said after a moment. 'Of course Norman left me something.'

'He didn't,' Maurice said again, this time in a tone of great satisfaction. 'And you know he didn't.'

'I don't know anything of the sort,' said Susan.

Maurice really smiled this time. 'You were making all that up,' he said. 'You know what was in Father's will as well as I do. He left everything equally divided between Beryl and me, except for a few legacies. There was five hundred or so for Marabelle, I believe, and something for the Weinkrauts. And Father told us about it, because he gave us verbal instructions that we were always to look after you if you needed it.'

Susan turned away abruptly, took hold of the back of a chair and leant on it heavily.

'All right then,' she said, 'I'll tell you the real reason. It had nothing to do with the will. But Norman knew that I had killed Piers, and he knew why, and he—he threatened me that if I went on and broke up the marriage of—of this man I love, that he'd expose me. He promised that if I would go right away, he'd do his best to protect me, but that if I stayed here, he'd give me away to the police.'

'But look here,' said Sholto, bouncing up and down on the sofa, 'how does that fit with his trying to make you and me get married again? Did he think he could send me away too?'

'No,' said Susan, 'but if we were married, then the—the danger to this other marriage would be over, wouldn't it?'

'Certainly not,' said Sholto.

'Oh heavens,' cried Susan, clenching her hands, 'do I have to explain it *all*? Can't I be spared anything? Don't you understand, Norman thought that you knew that I'd killed Piers, and he realised that if we were married, you wouldn't have to give evidence against me?'

'Me?' said Sholto. 'But why ever should he have thought that?'

'From the extraordinary way you behaved as soon as you knew of the murder, of course.'

'Extraordinary?' said Sholto touchily. 'What was extraordinary about it?'

'Why, dashing straight up to the inspector and telling him that you were the murderer,' said Susan.

'But I didn't,' said Sholto. 'I only told him he'd better arrest me because all the evidence was against me.'

'Anyway, Norman thought you were doing it to protect me,' said Susan.

'Good God!' said Sholto unbelievingly.

Then he began to look rather pleased with himself. 'But Norman always saw the best in every one, didn't he? He saw that streak in me. He realised that there were potentialities for self-sacrifice—'

The inspector interrupted before Sholto could embark on a lecture on his own nature. 'Mrs Beltane, this man you've told us about, this man you hope to marry—would you mind telling me who he is?'

Sholto looked at me. Maurice looked back at the carpet. Susan drew a deep breath and then raised her eyes to the inspector. Suddenly it was more than I could bear, and I jumped up and ran out of the room.

I ran upstairs. I ran into my bedroom and locked the door. I dropped on the bed and burst into a wild fit of weeping. Darkness covered the earth, and loneliness and utter desolation. Then I knew that I was going to murder Susan.

But first I was going to take my own photograph of John out of my bag and tear it into very small pieces and stamp on them. I reached for my bag. But it was not on the dressing-table, where I was sure I had left it. It was on a chair beside the dressing-table. I opened it and looked for the photograph. It was not there.

I believe that for a moment I thought that Mrs Fawcett had stolen my photograph of John along with Beryl's photograph of

Norman. The world seemed to be full of disappearing pictures. Then I came to my senses and laughed and then began to cry again, some of the pleasantest tears that I have ever known. Then I sat down on the bed, lit a cigarette and began to think out what must actually have happened.

It must have been when Maurice came home and refused to say where he had been at the time of Piers' murder. That had made Susan believe that Maurice was the murderer. She had probably thought that his motive had been connected with Beryl and the advances that Piers had made to her. So Susan had decided to draw suspicion to herself.

First she had supplied herself with a photograph of a possible fourth husband, intending to let the inspector catch a glimpse of this at some suitable moment. I remembered how she had left the photograph lying on the floor just long enough for the inspector to see it, and then had swept it up into her bag. But she had meant to explain to me what she was doing, and would have done so if Sholto had not walked into the room when he did.

By the time that I had thought this out, I had calmed down and was feeling an unaccustomed affection for Susan. I remembered her as she had been when we were children, always pushing me around, helping herself to my possessions, but always fiercely protecting me against the outer world. That

238

was what she was trying to do now. She was trying desperately and tragically to protect her child from the danger that threatened him. The unfortunate thing was that Maurice was trying to do the same for her. They had formed themselves very efficiently into a Mutual Destruction Society.

I smoked my cigarette to the end and lit another from its stub. That was my last cigarette, unless by any chance there was one around loose in my bag. Picking it up again, I poked about inside it. As I was doing it, a new uneasiness took hold of me. I searched more anxiously, then emptied everything out on the bed. My brooch was gone.

It was a brooch of turquoises and garnets that I usually wore on the lapel of the suit in which I had come here. When I had decided to wear Ernst's rose, I had unpinned the brooch and dropped it into my bag. Now it was not there.

I was fond of it and I felt angry. At first I was angry with Susan, thinking that as she had been at my bag to steal my photograph, she had also taken the brooch. Then I realised that the two things were not in the same class. Susan would steal a photograph of one's husband, or even one's husband himself, if she really wanted him, but she would never steal Granny's brooch.

But perhaps Mrs Fawcett would.

I ran downstairs, interrupted the inspector

239

in something that he was saying to Maurice, and told him that a brooch had been stolen from my bag.

Rather to my surprise, for I had not really expected him to take much notice, he became very interested, broke off his questioning of Maurice, and made me describe the brooch in detail.

When I had finished, he said, 'Has any one else missed anything of value?'

'I've got nothing of value with me,' said Susan.

Sholto patted his pockets, revealed a row of five fountain-pens clipped inside his jacket, shook his head and said, 'Everything okay here.'

The inspector looked at Beryl. 'And you, Miss Rice?'

'I haven't looked,' she said. 'I've a few odds and ends of jewellery in my room, but I didn't think of looking at them.'

'Please go and see if they're all there.'

Beryl went out, and while she was gone, the inspector took a rest. One of his men came in and whispered to him, and he nodded, as if he had been told something that he had expected. In a few minutes, Beryl returned.

'My seed pearls are missing,' she said.

Susan said indignantly, 'Oh, that's really too bad. They were the only nice thing she had. But never mind, darling, I'll get you some more.'

Beryl shrugged her shoulders as if the loss

left her quite indifferent.

'A necklace?' said the inspector.

'A necklace, ear-rings and a bracelet,' said Beryl.

He nodded, rather satisfied than otherwise.

'I think we've identified your Mrs Fawcett for you,' he said, 'and I don't think we'll be long in picking her up. When we do, you may get your pearls back, Miss Rice.'

'Then there is something wrong about her?' I asked quickly. 'Didn't I tell you so?'

'There's something wrong about her,' he answered, 'but she isn't necessarily a poisoner. In fact, that's distinctly unlikely. She's never tried anything of the sort before.'

'But all those dead men...'

'Part of her stock-in-trade,' he said, 'along with her forged references. I dare say she acquired those photographs at a sale. But when I heard about them, I knew whom to look for, and we checked her finger-prints. She's a woman we've been looking for for some time, a certain Matilda Paul, wanted on several charges of larceny.'

'What about her husband?' I said.

'I don't think she ever had one.'

'Then why didn't she like having him mentioned? I shouldn't mind mentioning an imaginary husband.'

'Perhaps she thought you were asking too many questions. That may have decided her to move on, even before the murder.'

'Well, if I'd decided on being a thief like her,' I said, 'I should at least have learnt to cook. Her cooking was really the most suspicious thing about her.'

'Not in this country,' said Susan with a sigh. 'But, Inspector, don't you think it's possible that my husband—no, I mean Mr Rice—may have discovered what she was, and that she murdered him because of that?'

'And Mr Beltane?' he asked.

'Perhaps Piers interfered in some way, or found out something concerning her plot against Norman. All along, Mr Dapple's been insisting that Piers' murder was secondary to that of Norman.'

The inspector nodded slowly. 'Yes ... The important motive to discover is the motive for Mr Rice's murder. I agree with Mr Dapple there. It was the more complicated murder and required the more careful planning. But still, Mrs Fawcett—or rather Matilda Paul—wasn't physically capable of murdering even a rather small man, like Mr Beltane, by hitting him on the head with a hammer. And she's never been known to use violence.' He looked round, as the man who had come in a few minutes ago reappeared.

The man said, 'We've just found something of interest in Matilda's fireplace.'

'What is it?'

'A quantity of broken glass. And there's more stuck away up the chimney. We're just

242

getting it down.'

The inspector got up and went out with him.

At that point I remembered that Susan was supposed to be trying to take my husband away from me. I began, 'Oh, Susan, about John—'

'Don't,' she implored. 'Not a word.'

'All right,' I said. 'But next time—'

'What *is* all this about John?' Maurice interrupted.

I wondered how soon I could take him on one side and clear the air for him, and perhaps find out incidentally where he really had been yesterday morning.

'Nothing,' said Susan. 'Nothing at all.'

'Broken glass,' said Sholto. 'Glass. What glass has been broken? Could it be a milk bottle?'

'Why on earth should it be?' said Susan contemptuously.

'I was just wondering if there could have been a practice attempt on Norman, or anything, in which a milk bottle got broken,' said Sholto.

'But that would mean that it *was* Mrs Fawcett,' I said.

'Oh, for heaven's sake be quiet about your Mrs Fawcett,' said Susan. 'You're only confusing things.'

Sholto nodded. 'An obvious red-herring, as I told you.'

'All right,' I said, 'so don't listen to me either

when I tell you what glass has obviously got broken.'

'Well, what?' said Susan.

'The glass over the Roger Clegg. And that's where the picture's gone now. She's off and away with it, probably rolled round her under her corsets.'

The inspector, coming in again, said, 'Looks as if you're right, Mrs Baynes. There are the broken pieces of a picture-frame and its glass, rolled up in a piece of newspaper, stuck away up the chimney in Matilda Paul's room. A few pieces of the glass had got loose and fallen down the chimney into the grate, and so attracted the sergeant's attention. I've never known Matilda trouble with pictures before, but she must have thought from all the fuss about it that it was something unusually valuable, and that since the rest of her haul was pretty poor, it was worth her while departing from her usual practice. Jewellery and cash are what she generally sticks to.'

'I hope I never see that picture again,' said Susan. 'Never, never.'

At that point I asked the inspector if there was any longer any serious objection to my making some coffee for every one or would he suspect that I was only trying to destroy evidence. He gave me permission to go ahead and I went out to the kitchen. Beryl came to help me, and we began by clearing up a little of the mess in the kitchen. While we were doing it, the milk-man arrived. He was escorted by a detective, who brought him and the milk bottles straight into the kitchen, and then took the man through it to have a talk with the inspector. The poor man looked scared out of his wits, as if he thought he was going to be accused of selling poisoned milk. A few minutes later, Basil arrived.

It was a pleasure to see someone who looked fresh and tidy, who had slept well and was not seriously troubled in spirit. Of course he did not know yet about Norman's death, and thought that the police had been on non-stop duty on account of the first murder.

'No rose for you this morning,' he said regretfully. 'Haven't they found out yet who did it?'

'Why?' I said. 'D'you think there'll be roses again when they do?'

'Well, there might be, mightn't there?' he said. 'I mean, you never know what queer things may be connected. But—'

'Stop,' I said excitedly. 'Wait!' I had just remembered the thoughts that had come to me the moment before Susan had spilled her handbag in front of me.

Basil stopped and waited, half-way to the scullery to change his trousers.

'Basil,' I said, my voice shaking a little as I began to understand the possibilities in my own question, 'when you arrived here yesterday, you found a rose on the window-ledge, didn't you?'

'Yes,' he said.

'And you brought it in?'

'Yes.'

'And you brought in the milk bottles?'

'Yes.'

'Now—think very carefully. Think very carefully indeed. Don't say anything at all that you don't feel absolutely certain about. But when you picked up Mr Rice's bottle of T.T. milk from the doorstep, was the gold cap intact or was there any kind of puncture in it?'

CHAPTER TWENTY-ONE

Basil obligingly thought very carefully. His thinking went on for some time, his blue eyes becoming deep pools of anxiety and his self-questioning, I had to assume from his expression, reaching depths of doubt and distrust of himself which it must have been cruel of me to stir.

At last he said, 'I'll have to go on thinking about it, if you don't mind. I'd like to get it right. I will get it if I go on thinking long enough. But I'll have to forget it first, and then it'll suddenly come to me. I'm like that.'

I accepted that and he went on into the scullery to change. When he came out again, I told him about Norman's death. He looked

246

upset and silently dived into the cupboard after the dust-pan and brush and the other things he wanted. Emerging he said, 'I suppose that clears it all up then. Did he leave a confession?'

'About what?' I asked.

'About the murder. Didn't he do the murder and then commit suicide?'

'It isn't generally thought so.'

'Queer,' he said. 'That's how it looks to me. But of course I don't know about these things. I'm awfully ignorant altogether. I hardly know anything.'

'Well, you see, Mr Rice was meaning to change his will,' I said. 'He'd even written a letter to his lawyer, telling him he wanted to see him later in the week. It was lying on his desk when we found him.'

'Well, people often do things the wrong way round,' said Basil, 'like a terrier we once had. I remember seeing him swallow a mouse and then go on looking for it.'

'Mr Rice wasn't a terrier.'

'No—but there's my brother-in-law too,' he said. 'He's the sort of man who drops his ash all over the carpet and then says, "Where's the ash-tray?" Or he says he'll make the tea, and he pours boiling water into the pot without having put any tea leaves into it.'

'I've done that myself,' I said.

'Then you see what I mean?'

'No.'

'Well, I'll tell you some other things my
247

brother-in-law does,' said Basil, warming up. 'He puts his dirty socks away in the drawer and sends his clean ones to the wash. And he sends cheques to people without signing them. And he goes and eats all the biscuits in the middle of the night, and then says at tea, "Why aren't there any biscuits?" And he takes mother's good cutting-out scissors to cut up pieces of linoleum, and then he takes them to cut his nails and says, "These scissors are blunt." And he—'

'Listen,' I said, 'I don't believe your brother-in-law has anything to do with this murder. It looks to me as if you want to make him the fall-guy, or whatever it's called, and I sympathise with you in the attempt, seeing the sort of man he seems to be, but I'm sure it won't work.'

'I only meant,' said Basil, 'that people do queer things. Because a thing seems queer, one shouldn't say it couldn't have happened. Now I'll go away and think about the milk bottles, Mrs Baynes. If I go on long enough, I'll remember what you want.'

He went out, and I went on making coffee and toast and trying to think out what it would mean if the top of the milk bottle had been punctured while it was still on the doorstep.

The first thing it would mean was that Ernst was the murderer. It would mean that he had come over, bringing a rose with him to disguise the real purpose of his visit, had looked into the

248

kitchen to make sure that there was no one there who might suddenly open the back door and catch him, had stuck some instrument through the top of the bottle, and had squirted the powdered-up drug into the milk.

It would mean too that he had intended to commit the murder a day sooner, but on that day, when he looked cautiously into the kitchen, he had seen me there, getting the breakfast, and rather than risk my interrupting him in his delicate operation on the milk bottle, he had tapped on the window, presented me with the rose and talked to me.

The motive was simple enough. There was a legacy for him in Norman's will.

But the puzzling thing was the second rose. Why had he left it behind on the window-sill, thus advertising the fact that he had been over to the kitchen?

I was worrying about this, wondering if it could have been mere carelessness, or if he had been afraid someone might have seen him and so had thought it best to leave the rose as an innocent explanation of his visit, when I heard a slight sound at the window, and there was Ernst's face, close to the glass, smiling at me, while he tapped gently at the pane with a rose.

For a moment I was petrified, so full of my own thoughts and fears that I could scarcely realise that he was a human being, and not some terrifying creation of my own imagination. Then I went to the door. I opened it and said curtly, 'Come in.'

He looked at me anxiously, holding out the rose, 'Aren't you vell?' he asked.

'Of course I'm well. Why shouldn't I be well?' I did not take the rose.

'Vell, when you looked at me I thought you vere just going to be sick or something.' Looking a little offended, he laid the rose down on the table. 'Shouldn't I have come? Ve saw lights on everywhere in the night, and I wanted to make sure you were all right.'

He looked so friendly and so concerned that my fit of the horrors began to pass. 'Then you don't know about Norman?' I said.

'Norman?'

I told him what had happened. While I was speaking his face grew white, and as I finished he sat down abruptly. He stared straight in front of him.

'My poor friend,' he said in a low voice. 'My poor old friend.' There were tears in his eyes. Then he moved his head, looking at me uncertainly. 'Of course, it is a mercy really, but I don't suppose his murderer knew that ... They're sure it was murder?'

I told him about the letter to the lawyer and the saucepan.

He nodded and said, 'Yes, yes ...' Picking up his rose, he frowned at it as if he wondered what it was doing there.

'What did you mean about its being a mercy?' I asked.

'Oh, he had cancer, you know.'

'Cancer!'

'Yes,' said Ernst. 'You didn't know? He told me—I think he had to tell someone—and made me promise not to tell. You *are* sure it vas murder? In the circumstances, to kill Beltane and then himself…' He left it unfinished, eyeing me questioningly.

I had sat down too. What he had just told me made me feel that I did not want to talk any more. But I understood a good many things now that I had not understood before.

'I wish it were like that,' I said, 'but the will and the saucepan…' I stopped suddenly, thinking about the saucepan that had mysteriously got washed in the middle of the night, and realising, with a return of the fears of a moment ago, that someone might have got into the kitchen by the window. I glanced at it. It was securely fastened on the inside. 'Ernst,' I said, trying to sound casual, 'did you know what was in Norman's will?'

'Not in detail,' he said. 'He told me he had made me an executor, and I said it would be better if he made Millie, as she understands these things better than I do. And he said he vas leaving me something, and I said he had no need to do that. And he said if the children should vant to sell the furniture, they were to let Millie have first pick. But I think nothing is antique enough for Millie … Why are you asking me this?'

251

I did not have to answer, because just then Basil came hurrying into the kitchen. The anxiety had disappeared from his face.

'There wasn't any,' he said.

Ernst's face twitched nervously and he looked at the blithe youth as if he were something disagreeable that he had stepped in.

'No puncture,' Basil explained.

'You're quite sure?' I said.

Basil nodded his curly head several times. 'Yes, it came to me all of a sudden and I knew for certain. I notice things like that, you know, holes in people's heels, or scratches in polish, or any of the things that oughtn't to be there. So once I could get my mind round to it, I knew that I should have noticed a hole in the top of the milk bottle if there'd been one when I picked it up off the doorstep, and there wasn't.'

Ernst looked from him to me.

'Ah ... I understand,' he said slowly. 'The milk bottle on the doorstep, my rose on the vindow-sill, your face when you saw me this morning, your questions about Norman's vill ...'

'I've been suspecting everybody,' I said apologetically.

Ernst nodded. 'Yes, of course. And that's quite right. But how could I have killed Piers Beltane? And vy should I have done so?'

'I hadn't really worked it out,' I said. 'I suppose you might think he'd seen you at the milk bottle, and I suppose you could have

252

hidden in the cloakroom, waiting for him.'

'Only how could I have known it vould be Piers who vould come into the cloakroom and not somebody else, and how could I have done it when I vas at the Observatory? It's true I could have murdered Norman, but I could not have murdered Piers except with the help of a miracle.'

'I know,' I said, 'I hadn't thought it out properly. In a way, the difficulty is to fit the two murders together. Sholto's been saying all along that Piers must have been murdered simply because he walked in and saw somebody in the cloakroom who wasn't supposed to be there, and when Norman was murdered, Sholto said we now knew what the person had been hiding there for—it was to get at the milk to put the poison into it. And that couldn't have been you, because you'd have been able to poison the milk without coming into the house—'

'Of course, if it had been my brother-in-law,' Basil interrupted, 'it would have been the other way round.'

'Oh dear,' I said, 'his brother-in-law again. He'll hang the poor man before he's finished. What would have been the other way round?'

'Well, if my brother-in-law had done some simple thing which he thought was going to annoy people,' said Basil, 'and for some reason he thought it worth while to try and cover it up—not that he would usually, he doesn't care

253

what any one thinks of him, particularly me—still, if he did, he'd cover it up by doing something much worse and much more complicated. For instance, if he dropped some butter on the carpet, he'd try to take the stain out with petrol and then drop his cigarette on it and set the carpet and the whole house on fire. See what I mean? It's like a dog we had once that used to dig holes in the flower-beds and chew up the door-mat. Those were his two special crimes that he was always getting punished for. And when he'd done both, he used to drag the mat on top of the hole to hide it.'

'Basil's dogs and brothers-in-law had better take over this case,' I said. 'He's determined to get them mixed up in it somehow . . .' I stopped. I had just taken the boiling kettle off the stove and because of the startled movement I made, a good deal of the water splashed on to the floor. Some of it sprayed my ankles, but I hardly noticed the sting. 'Basil, did you *mean* something when you said that?' I demanded.

'Of course,' he said. 'It's what I've told my sister over and over again. A man like that isn't any good. She ought to divorce him.'

'No,' I said, 'did you mean anything—special?'

He gave me a puzzled look, and I realised that he had no idea that he had just told me who the murderer was.

254

CHAPTER TWENTY-TWO

I felt an intense and rather horrible excitement. But I knew that I must think this out before I said anything about it to any one. I spent the next few minutes in a daze, only half aware that I was putting spoonfuls of coffee in a jug and heating up some milk in a saucepan.

I came a little way out of the daze to hear Basil saying, 'By the way, I do like that paint in the hall, I think I'll do my own room in that colour.' I remembered then that I had never paid him for the paint. I asked him how much it had cost and he told me, but said there was no hurry about it. However, I turned away from the stove, letting the milk boil over a little, opened my bag and paid him.

As he pocketed the money, he said, 'But I suppose it'll never be finished now.'

'What?' I asked.

'The painting in the hall. I'd come along and help in the evening if you'd like it. I've a client in the afternoon whom I couldn't let down— she always plays Chopin to me while I work— but I could come along afterwards. Only I suppose you won't be going on with it.'

I shook my head. 'I'm afraid it'll never be finished. Thanks all the same.' Then a new and confusing thought came into my head and I picked up my bag again and looked hurriedly inside it. I counted the money in it. There were nearly three pounds, which was just about the amount that should have been there. But that didn't make sense, because it was Mrs Fawcett's habit to steal valuables *and cash*. She had taken my brooch: she ought to have taken my money.

So again I started thinking about Mrs Fawcett, and gradually, with my new knowledge of the identity of the murderer, I began to piece the whole story together. It came out quite differently from anything that I had thought of before. But there were no flaws in it that I could see.

I do not know how I got through the next half-hour. I was not conscious of having made a plan, yet I acted without hesitation, as if I had thought out in detail everything I had to do.

The first thing was to make the breakfast, and to have my own hurriedly, so that when I called every one else into the kitchen, I could say that I had already finished and was going up to my room. Unluckily this did not work. When I went to the kitchen door and called out loudly that breakfast was ready only Susan and Beryl appeared. There was no sign of Sholto.

Susan fell on the food, complaining that I might for once have made something besides toast, since she was ravenous. But Beryl closed her pale lips tightly and shook her head. Susan tried to make her eat, but Beryl went on refusing. Leaving them to fight it out between themselves, I muttered that I wanted a wash and went upstairs, as unobtrusively as I could.

I suppose I might have gone to the inspector. Perhaps that is what I ought to have done. But I wanted to have proof in my hands before I went to him with any more theories, and I knew where I could find proof.

I had reached the first landing when I realised that Beryl was following me. When she saw that I had seen her, she came up to me quickly.

'What are you doing?' she asked.

'I'm going to get dressed,' I said.

'I mean, really,' she said impatiently. 'You slipped out of the kitchen as if you were hurrying off to dispose of a corpse.'

'Nothing of the sort,' I said. 'I was just—'

'You're up to something.' Her voice was astonishingly stern. There was more force in her than I had realised. 'I think I'll come along with you.'

'All right,' I said, 'come into my room and watch me dress.'

She followed me into my room, but as soon as the door was shut, she said again, 'You're up to something, Marabelle. Come on, tell me what it is.'

'Well, I want to check up on something,' I said. 'And since you're here you can answer a question. D'you know when your photograph of Norman disappeared?'

'I'm not quite sure,' she said. 'I didn't miss it till this morning, but it must have been gone earlier. If Mrs Fawcett cleared out around nine or ten last night, she must have taken it during the evening.'

'Then you didn't miss it when you went up to bed last night?'

'I don't remember.'

'Think!' I begged.

'I was so tired,' she said, 'I just tumbled into bed and turned out the light. And then I couldn't sleep, so I came down...'

'But haven't you any idea if the photograph was in its usual place or not?'

'It can't have been, can it?'

'Don't think about that,' I said. 'Forget any one ever said anything to you about Mrs Fawcett. Just try to visualise your room any time yesterday when you went into it. Which is the first occasion when you're certain the picture was missing?'

'This morning,' she said.

'Then it could have been there when you went to bed last night?'

'It could have been—but I don't think it was.'

'Just because of what you've been told about Mrs Fawcett, or because you're beginning to remember an image of the room earlier?'

She shook her head helplessly. 'I don't know, I really don't. What's all this about, anyway?'

'I'm not quite sure,' I said. 'But I don't think Mrs Fawcett took your photograph, or my brooch, or the Clegg. I think she was much too frightened by the first murder to take anything. I think she just bundled a few of her own belongings into a bag and did a bolt while she had the chance. You see, my brooch was taken from my bag, but my money wasn't—and you'd think that in the circumstances, unprepared for a sudden flitting, she'd have grabbed any money she could get.'

'Then who took your brooch—and why?'

'I think someone took it who had never stolen things before. Someone who in the ordinary way would never dream of taking sixpence that didn't belong to him. Someone who was only thinking of confusing the trail leading to his conviction as a murderer. Someone who, for his own reasons, wanted to keep the Clegg, yet to make us think Mrs Fawcett had taken it along with one or two other things we were sure to miss. Someone who strewed a little broken glass around in Mrs Fawcett's fireplace, so that the fragments of the frame which he had stuck up the chimney were sure to be discovered—'

She stopped me with a hand that closed tightly on my wrist.

'Where are these things now?' she asked in a low voice.

'I think I know, roughly speaking,' I said. 'I'm going to look for them.'

259

'I'll come with you,' she said.

'I'd rather you didn't.'

She was stubborn. 'I'm coming.'

'All right,' I said, 'but it may take some time. I've an idea I can find the Clegg fairly easily, but the other things may be anywhere. The photograph may even have been destroyed, and your pearls and my brooch may be in someone's pocket. But if we can find the Clegg, we've got what we need.'

'Why?' she said. 'What will it prove?'

'I think it'll help in tangling the murderer up in his own clues,' I said. 'Come along, if you really want to.'

'Where to?'

'The attic.'

The look she gave me then was frightened, as if at that point she would sooner have withdrawn. But she came with me when I went along the passage, and I heard her breathing unevenly behind me as we went up the stairs. I wished I could send her back, because her nervousness infected me.

I was hoping that we would find the attic empty, but at the sound we made on the stairs, Sholto came running out to meet us. I tried to look natural, to give nothing away. I need not have bothered. Sholto was not in a noticing mood. His face was very red, and his eyes had a glassy brilliance.

'I've been all wrong, I've been all wrong from the beginning!' he cried. 'I've had the motive all wrong. I thought I understood what was happening, but I didn't. Oh God, Marabelle—' He clutched my arm. 'I'm in frightful danger.'

I trembled when he touched me, but not knowing what else to do, I tried to play up to him. For the moment it seemed the only thing to do.

'You're always so dramatic,' I said. 'What's the trouble now?'

'Dramatic? I'm the calmest person in this house,' he cried. 'I'm the only one with any sense. And I tell you what I'm doing. I'm getting out of it. I'm getting out of it as fast as I can.'

'But what's happened?' I asked.

His eyes glared. 'You'll see,' he said. 'You'll find out, like I did. But let me advise you, get out quick.'

I nodded. 'Yes, of course. That's what I want to do. But d'you think the police will let you go?'

'The police! I'm not waiting to ask the police, I'm clearing out before any one can stop me. God, how I wish I'd stayed at home. I never meant to get mixed up in anything like this. It's awful!' He sounded as if he were near tears.

'Well, go along,' I said, and made room so that he could pass me on the stairs. Beryl, below me, pressed herself flat against the banisters as if she were scared of him. 'Somehow I don't think you'll get far,' I added.

261

'I don't care how far I get so long as I get out of this house,' he said. 'I thought I knew what he was up to, but I didn't, I had it all wrong. I didn't realise that I was in danger too—deadly danger. A clean sweep, that's what he wants. Now let me past.' His headlong rush down the stairs was so fast that I felt sure he must fall, but he reached the bottom safely and I heard his feet pounding down the lower flight.

My heart was beating so hard that I stood still for a moment before going on.

In a whisper, gazing down after Sholto, Beryl said, 'I don't understand. What scared him?'

'He wasn't scared,' I said. 'Come along, let's get on.'

'But what did he mean, Marabelle?' She came up quickly beside me and clutched my arm. 'Why's he in danger?'

'He isn't—that's to say, not from the direction he wanted us to think. Don't you realise, Sholto's the murderer?'

For a moment she seemed to doubt that I meant what I said, then she let go of my arm and sat down on one of the boxes that were strewn around the attic. She pressed her hands against her temples. 'When did you know?' she asked.

'It was something that Basil said about his brother-in-law,' I said. 'He said that if his brother-in-law spilled some butter on the carpet, he'd try to get the spot out by using petrol and setting the carpet and perhaps the whole house on fire. A simple crime concealed by a worse and more complicated one. And it was Sholto, wasn't it, who kept trying to make us all think that Piers had been murdered because he had somehow interfered with the murder of Norman, which had been carefully planned. And that made us look for the motives for murdering Norman rather than Piers. And Sholto had no reason to murder Norman.'

'But why should he murder Piers?'

'He hated him.'

'Was that all?'

'I think it's the best motive there is. And I shouldn't wonder if it was the strongest feeling Sholto's ever had in his life. I don't think he'd planned to kill Piers, but when Piers walked into the cloakroom and Sholto suddenly saw the hammer, the temptation must have been more than he could stand.'

'But he accused himself straight off,' said Beryl.

'Knowing that he wouldn't be believed. As Susan always said, though I never used to believe her, Sholto's very intelligent. I think he was already planning Norman's murder then, simply to change the apparent meaning of the first murder.'

'And he took my photograph and my pearls?'

'Yes—because he wanted the Clegg. He

263

wanted it to annoy Susan, just as a part of his revenge. I suppose he'd seen Mrs Fawcett slip out of the house, and thought that if he took several things, she'd be blamed for stealing them all. But he was just too honest to take my money. That's where he blundered ... What did you say?' For I thought she had started to say something.

But she shook her head and did not speak. She was looking at me thoughtfully, frowning as if she did not quite believe what I had said.

'Well, let's get on,' I said. 'The Clegg's in here somewhere. I'll find it if it takes me all day.'

I had no idea at that moment where I was going to begin, and if there is an occupation I detest, it is looking for things. As a rule, if I lose something, I prefer to let it stay lost rather than dig around through dusty heaps of paper or behind heavy boxes that have to be tugged inch by inch away from the wall so that I can look behind them. But to-day the job had to be done. There was no choice.

In fact it turned out to be far simpler than I had expected. I was looking round when my eye fell on the rolls of linoleum propped up in a row near the window. When I had seen them before they had reminded me of a row of organ pipes. But now they stood too crookedly to look like organ pipes. Someone had moved them since I had seen them last.

I walked across to them. A picture, I

264

thought, that had been taken out of its frame, could easily have been tucked away inside one of the rolls. I reached for the nearest.

I heard a choking sound from Beryl. The whole thing seemed suddenly to have become too much for her. Jumping up, she ran out of the room and I heard her running down the stairs, almost as fast as Sholto. In a way, I was glad, though something cold slid down my spine as I thought suddenly of being quite alone up there. I found I had to nerve myself to make the next movement.

I suppose I was clumsy. The roll slipped out of my hand and fell against the others. They all began to slide and fall. One, a very thick one, that looked as if it might have enough linoleum in it to cover a whole room, fell with a heavy thud.

The room began to go black. I think I screamed.

Sticking out of the end of the roll of linoleum was a pair of feet in felt slippers.

CHAPTER TWENTY-THREE

I have never quite fainted in my life. But I have had patches of unconsciousness during which I have somehow managed to get from one place to another without any knowledge of the process. At one moment I have been in one

265

spot, and at the next, without any interval whatever, so far as my own mind has been able to tell me, I have been yards away.

I have an uneasy feeling that if I investigated how this is done, I might get involved in the quantum theory or something of that sort. I do not think I should enjoy this, as I have no talent for mathematics, so perhaps it will be best for my comfort to leave the phenomenon unexplored. At any rate, when the roll of linoleum fell over, I immediately found myself in a state of collapse on the landing below. The inspector was holding me up with an arm round my waist, while Sholto's face, still red and glassy-eyed, hovered before me.

I gave another good scream when I saw it.

'It's all right,' said the inspector casually. 'He isn't the murderer.'

'How d'you know?'

'Because I know who is.'

'How d'you know you know?'

'Here,' said Sholto, 'have some of this, and don't make such a fuss.'

I discovered then that the smell of whisky did not all come from him, but partly from the glass that he was holding under my nose. I gulped and began to feel more lucid.

'Now, I'd like to ask you just what you've been up to,' said the inspector.

'I'd like to sit down, then, if you don't mind,' I said.

He nodded and piloted me into my room.

Sholto waited hopefully in the doorway, but since neither the inspector nor I invited him to come in, he went away.

'Now,' said the inspector, closing the door, 'what took you up there?'

'Basil's brother-in-law,' I said.

'Of course. Basil's brother-in-law, just what I was expecting. And what else?'

I was still feeling too dizzy to explain it very well. 'You'd better ask Basil about it,' I said. I was aware of a great deal of tramping about going on upstairs. 'Have you been upstairs yourself?'

'Yes, I was going up just as you came down,' he said. 'Mr Dapple, whom some of the men intercepted in the road, and whose first idea seems to have been to get away from the house as fast as he could, had some thoughts and told us what he'd found here.'

Here was an opportunity to find something out. 'You say you saw me on the stairs,' I said. 'What did I look like?'

'Pretty awful,' he said. 'Can't say I blame you. But what I want to know is, did you know what you were going to find?'

'No,' I said, 'I thought I was going to find the Clegg.'

'You would have,' he said, 'if you'd gone on looking.'

'You mean it's there with—her?'

He nodded. 'Now then, why did you go upstairs?'

I found it extraordinary difficult now to remember exactly how I had reasoned out that the Clegg must be in the attic, but I told him as well as I could.

He nodded again and said, 'It was a good point about the money that wasn't taken. I ought to have thought of it, but I wasn't bothering much about Mrs Fawcett.'

'I know,' I said. 'I kept telling everybody they ought to think more about her. Not that I see how that helps now, but surely, surely, Inspector, Sholto Dapple's the murderer.'

'In that case, how did he wash up the saucepan that had had the poisoned milk in it, while you were keeping guard with your paint pots in the hall?'

'Perhaps he got down a drain-pipe and in at the kitchen window.'

'And out of the window and up again?'

'Well, perhaps.'

'Was the kitchen window unlatched in the morning.'

'No,' I said, remembering that the window had certainly been fastened when Ernst appeared at it with his rose. 'All the same, when I met Sholto up in the attic just now, I was scared stiff. I was sure he was the murderer. He said a lot of things about being in deadly danger himself, but I thought that was just Sholto talking—besides, of course, trying to throw dust in our eyes.'

'No,' said the inspector, 'he was talking

sense for once.'

'I don't get it,' I said. 'What did he mean?'

'He meant that someone had chosen him as the scapegoat. We were all to think what you've been thinking.'

'But why should any one do that?'

'Well, it looks to me as if someone or other has something pretty serious against all the men your sister marries.'

I started to say something and then could not remember what it was that I had meant to say. The inspector gave a tired yawn. Thinking about the yawn, and how it meant that he knew his job was almost done, I almost forgot what he had said. But then it came back to me with a jolt.

'If you're still thinking that I washed up that saucepan, or had anything against Piers, or Norman, or Sholto—'

He made an irritable gesture, stopping me. 'No, in a way you've been the best suspect all along, and it would have saved me a lot of trouble if I could have found a convincing motive—for instance, your acute antagonism to your sister. You might have been trying to destroy everything she valued. Only in any sort of a crisis you seemed to stand by her. For instance, when she was trying to show that she herself had a motive for the murders, in order to draw suspicion away from her son, you made no protest at her using a photograph of your husband.'

'I was too frightened to protest,' I said. 'It might all have been true.'

'You didn't really think so.'

'Well, I did and I didn't.'

'And, anyway, it was you yourself who insisted that the saucepan had been washed up at a time that was really very inconvenient for you,' he said. 'It would have been far less suspicious if you'd admitted washing it up earlier. No, I haven't given you very much serious thought. The person I thought about most, from the moment when he turned up, was young Rice.'

'But it can't have been Maurice!' I saw that I had got to pull myself together, or something terrible might happen. 'He couldn't have washed up the saucepan, and he couldn't have murdered Mrs Fawcett. And I'm sure that when you look into his alibi for the morning, you'll find he was attending a lecture at the Imperial College, or doing something else that was perfectly normal. Any fool could see that he suspected Susan and was trying to protect her.'

'Yes—and that's just what this fool thought at first,' he said. 'But you know, young Rice must have seen, as well as you and I, that his mother was lying very fast and very badly to protect him. Yet he went on refusing to say anything.'

'Then—*was* it Maurice?'

With another stifled yawn, he said, 'Mr

270

Dapple has been trying to make me think it was. He's had him picked as the murderer all along. But as you say, Rice can't have murdered Mrs Fawcett, because he couldn't have got in or out of the house without being seen, except during those few minutes yesterday evening, when our man followed you across to the Weinkrauts'. And the murder of Mrs Fawcett, the hiding of her body and the stealing of the various articles that disappeared, took time. No, Rice wasn't the murderer. And he knew his mother wasn't either. Yet he was trying to draw suspicion to himself to protect the person who was.'

'But—' I knew what he was going to say, yet I had to protest. 'But it *can't* have been...'

'Think,' he said. 'Who must have known, by the sound of footsteps in the night that she recognised, that Piers Beltane and her mother had arrived here? Who must have gone off to her work, uneasy in mind about it, wondering what was going to happen? Who wasn't sure if she was in love with her mother's husband, or hated him for his disloyalty, and for the disloyalty she had almost committed herself? Who had a good deal of hatred against him, in any case, because of the injury to her own father? Who could easily have slipped away from her work on a large market-garden without being seen, come back on her bicycle, gone into the cloakroom to take off her wet coat, and there been surprised by Piers Beltane, going in there to plant the Clegg, in order to make it appear that her father had stolen it?'

He paused, looking as if he expected me to answer. I said nothing. He went on, 'We don't know what happened there. Perhaps Beltane made love to her. Perhaps he didn't, and it was that that roused her rage. But she killed him and escaped. Later, when she was sent for, she returned. Then, in the evening when she took some supper up to Mrs Fawcett, the old woman must have approached her and told her that she knew she had been in the house during the morning. Almost certainly Mrs Fawcett demanded money. But the girl's tall and strong, and Mrs Fawcett was a little old woman. I think they were in Mrs Fawcett's room, and the girl smothered her with pillows from the bed. That's how the old woman was killed. I don't think the girl thought at once of incriminating Dapple, because when she took your brooch and some of her own jewellery, she must have been meaning us to think that Mrs Fawcett had stolen them and cleared out. I don't know if she hid the body in the attic straight away, or whether it was only when her mother asked her to bring her things down from it and to take Dapple's upstairs, and she found the Clegg under his bed, that she thought of hiding the body and the picture together, so that when they were found, Dapple was sure to be suspected. But that's what she did, and this morning, when she

272

realised that you were going up to the attic to search, she went with you to watch what happened. And that's why I'm telling you all this. I want to know what she did while you were both up there.'

I shut my eyes. I did not want to look at his face. But when I shut my eyes I immediately saw Beryl's, as it had looked when she saw me stretch out my hand towards the rolls of linoleum. She had known what I was going to find and suddenly she had not been able to bear it. She had run as if all hell were after her.

'And after all,' the inspector was adding wearily, 'she could have washed up that saucepan—in fact, that's probably why she came down to help you paint. She must have slipped in there when your back was turned for a moment.'

'But it's impossible!' I cried. 'Beryl loved her father. She might have killed Piers. She might have wanted to incriminate Sholto. I didn't know she hated Sholto so much, but still he's the one who first broke up their home and took her mother away from them all. But she loved her father, and she'd never have killed him.'

'Even if she knew he was dying of cancer?'

He gave a long sigh. 'I think her love for her father was behind all three killings—yes, all three, because during these last weeks she must have seen him several times in the grip of unbearable pain, and that's a very difficult thing for a young person to bear. So she

273

poisoned him mercifully and avenged him ...
Well?'

I still said nothing, so he went out and left
me.

CHAPTER TWENTY-FOUR

And that is nearly the end of it, except that the
inspector was wrong.

Beryl had not washed up the saucepan. I
knew that. I could not prove it, but I knew that
she had never been in the kitchen alone, and
that when we had both been in there together,
she had never touched the saucepan.

Beryl had not known her father had cancer.
The only person, other than the doctor, who
had known that, was Ernst Weinkraut.

Beryl had not murdered anybody.

Yet when I had reached out towards the rolls
of linoleum, she had known what I was going
to find, and later that day, when she found
herself hemmed in by terrifying circumstantial
evidence, she broke down and told us how she
had known. Until then, I believe, she had been
hoping that the truth would never be
discovered. She said that if Sholto had in fact
been accused of the murders she would have
told what she knew, but that she had believed
there was a possibility of nothing being solved,
in which case she would never have betrayed

274

her father. I do not think she quite understood that he had intended that Susan should be hanged for his murder and that of Piers, and that the baffling features of Norman's death came from his efforts to make his own suicide appear as murder.

For of course it was Susan that Norman had meant to involve, not Sholto. At the time when Norman had taken Mrs Fawcett's body up to the attic—it had happened while I was over at the Weinkrauts'—the attic had been Susan's bedroom. Beryl, going up there to fetch her mother's things, had seen him rolling up the body in the linoleum. He had not known she had seen him, and she had been too frightened to tell him. When later he was found dead, Beryl had not for a moment doubted, in spite of the puzzling evidence of the letter and the saucepan, that he had killed himself. She did not understand the motive for Mrs Fawcett's murder, but thought it must mean that it was he who had killed Piers, and that this had unhinged his mind.

Perhaps this was not far from the truth. I think that when he was in the cloakroom, taking off his coat, and when Piers walked in with the Clegg, and Norman saw how his years of forbearance were being repaid, something snapped in his mind.

I don't want to write a dissertation on the dangers of repressed jealousy, but I think that must have come in. And of course, he was a

275

dying man, and reckless. Besides that, Piers' use of the Roger Clegg must have seemed an unforgiven taunt. The Clegg was the one thing that Norman had tried to make Susan give him, and she had refused it. It may have been the sight of the picture in Piers' hands that tipped Norman over the edge. After all, he may have loved the Clegg better than he had ever loved Susan. I have sometimes wondered lately, if, in fact, he had ever loved her at all. She might have grown into a different person if he had.

The police later proved by the evidence of some hair that they found, that Norman had smothered Mrs Fawcett in his own bedroom. She must have gone in there during the evening, while he was lying down, perhaps in severe pain, and made her attempt at blackmail. The theft of the jewellery was to make us believe that Mrs Fawcett had taken it and gone, so that no thorough search would be made in the house until after he was dead. I do not know when he found the picture in the room that at that time had been Sholto's. I dare say Norman actually saw Sholto come back from the Weinkrauts' with the picture, and collected it from under Sholto's bed as soon as Sholto had left the room. Norman had never had any intention of changing his will. His talk about it and the letter to his lawyer had been to make us all sure that he had no intention of ending his life. Susan was to be accused of his murder. That in the end was how she was to pay.

I went home that same evening. Susan did not seem to want me there any longer. She wanted most to be alone with Beryl and Maurice. Sholto and I travelled back to London and separated at Victoria. I took a taxi home. The first thing I noticed when I opened the door was a curious smell. All of a sudden I realised that I was coming home to piles of washing-up that had been standing about since the Saturday before. It was the last straw.

Then I saw John. He came out of the kitchen with a desperate expression on his face, for he too had just come back and taken a look at the kitchen. But when he saw me he took me in his arms and kissed me and told me to go straight to bed and said that he would do the washing-up, and it all felt wonderful. I went to bed as he told me, and felt rather guilty because I thought he must be tired himself, and disappointed at having his conference interrupted. He had come back by plane when he got my cable and on reaching London had telephoned Susan and been told that I was on my way home. But presently a thought struck me, I called out, 'John!'

He came into the bedroom with his hands dripping.

'John, d'you realise that if I'd had the habit of doing the washing-up at the right time, Beryl or even poor old Sholto might have been hanged for murder?'

'Tell me later,' he said.

He went back to the kitchen.

But what I had said was true. If I had washed the milk-saucepan after I had used it, I do not know what might have happened. But as it was, the only person who could have washed that saucepan was Norman. He had stepped out of the study window, gone round to the back door and let himself into the kitchen with a key, washed the saucepan while Beryl and I were painting in the hall, gone back to the study by the way he had come, and then taken the poison. It had never been in the milk at all. His grimace, when he drank it, had been part of his plan, and he had washed the saucepan to conceal the fact that there had never been any poison in it.

Listening to John splashing about and cursing in the kitchen, I thought that perhaps there might be some sort of faintly comforting moral for me in that conclusion.

We hope you have enjoyed this Large Print book. Other Chivers Press or G.K. Hall & Co. Large Print books are available at your library or directly from the publishers.

For more information about current and forthcoming titles, please call or write, without obligation, to:

Chivers Press Limited
Windsor Bridge Road
Bath BA2 3AX
England
Tel. (01225) 335336

OR

G.K. Hall
P.O. Box 159
Thorndike, Maine 04986
USA
Tel. (800) 223–2336

All our Large Print titles are designed for easy reading, and all our books are made to last.